THE
WORKS
OF
LOVE

WRIGHT MORRIS

UNIVERSITY OF NEBRASKA PRESS
LINCOLN

THE

WORKS

OF

LOVE

International Standard Book Number 0–8032–5767–8

Library of Congress Catalog Card Number 51–11978

First Bison Book printing: September 1972

Most recent printing shown by the first digit below:

2   3   4   5   6   7   8   9   10

For

LOREN COREY EISELEY

&

to the memory of

SHERWOOD ANDERSON

pioneer in the works of love

Grown old in Love from Seven till Seven
*   times Seven*
I oft have wished for Hell for Ease from
*   Heaven.*

—WILLIAM BLAKE

We cannot bear connection. That is our
malady.

—D. H. LAWRENCE

If the word love *comes up between them I*
am lost.

—STENDHAL

Contents

IN THE WILDERNESS

1

IN THE dry places, men begin to dream. Where
the rivers run sand, there is something in man
that begins to flow. West of the 98th Meridian—
where it sometimes rains and it sometimes doesn't
—towns, like weeds, spring up when it rains, dry
up when it stops. But in a dry climate the husk of
the plant remains. The stranger might find, as if
preserved in amber, something of the green life that
was once lived there, and the ghosts of men who
have gone on to a better place. The withered towns
are empty, but not uninhabited. Faces sometimes
peer out from the broken windows, or whisper
from the sagging balconies, as if this place—now
that it is dead—had come to life. As if empty it is
forever occupied. One of these towns, so the story
would have it, was Indian Bow.

creativity?
or
nothingness
can
cripple
imagination

According to the record, a man named Will Brady was born on a river without water, in a sod house, near the trading post of Indian Bow. In time he grew to be a man who neither smoked, drank, gambled, nor swore. A man who headed no cause, fought in no wars, and passed his life unaware of the great public issues—it might be asked: why trouble with such a man at all? What is there left to say of a man with so much of his life left out? Well, there are women, for one thing—men of such caliber leave a lot up to the women—but in the long run Will Jennings Brady is there by himself. That might be his story. The man who was more or less by himself.

His father, Adam Brady, a lonely man, living in the sod house without a dog or a woman, spoke of the waste land around Indian Bow as God's country. It was empty. That was what he meant. If a man came in, he soon left on the next caboose. As a pastime, from the roof of his house, Adam Brady took potshots at the cupola, or at the rear platform, where the brakeman's lantern hung. He never hit anything. In his opinion, God's country should be like that.

Adam Brady's sod house was like a mound, or a storm cave, and after the first big snow of the winter just the snout, like a reluctant ground hog, could be seen peering out. The rest of the year it looked like the entrance to an abandoned mine. On the long winter nights the coyotes would gather to howl on the roof, or scratch their backs on the long-horns put up there to frighten them off. In the spring their tracks could be seen around the door, where the earth was soft.

Adam Brady spent several winters in this house alone. But one windy fall, with the winter looming, he put on his dark suit, his wide-brimmed hat, his military boots from the Confederate army, and rode eighty miles east in search of a photographer. He found one in the up-and-coming town of Callo-way. The picture shows Brady standing, hat in hand, with a virgin forest painted in behind him, and emerging from this forest a coyote and a one-eyed buffalo. The great humped head is there, but the rest of the beast is behind the screen.

This picture might have given any woman pause, but there was no indication, anywhere in it, of the landscape through the window that Adam Brady faced. There was not an inkling of the desolation of the empty plain. No hint of the sky, immense and faded, such as one might see in a landscape of China —but without the monuments that indicated men had passed, and might still be there. In that place, remote as it was, men at least had found time to carve a few idols, and others had passed either in order to worship, or to mutilate them. But in this place—this desolation out the window—what was there? Nothing but the sky that pressed on the earth with the dead weight of the sea, and here and there a house such as a prairie dog might have made.

Adam Brady had ten prints made of this picture, and six of them he mailed to old friends in Ohio; four he passed out to strangers, traveling men, that is, on their way east. A man who wanted a woman had to advertise for her, as he did for a cow. And a woman who wanted a man might be led to forget—for the time being—that great virgin forests are not, strictly speaking, part of the plains. That one-eyed buffaloes are seldom seen peering out of them. For there was some indication that the man in this picture lived in a real house, had friends and good neighbors, and perhaps a bay mare to draw a red-wheeled, green-tasseled gig. And that on Sunday afternoons he would drive his new wife down tree-lined roads. There was no indication that the man in the picture had on nearly everything that he owned, including a key-wind watch with a bent minute-hand. On the back of this picture, in a good hand, it was written that the man to be seen on the front, Adam Brady by name, was seeking a helpmate and a wife. And there was every indication that this man meant what he said.

What became of nine pictures there is no record, but the tenth, well thumbed and faded, with a

handlebar mustache added, finally got around to
Caroline Clayton, an Indiana girl. She was neither
a widow nor, strictly speaking, a girl any more.
Her independent cast of mind had not appealed to
the returning Civil War boys. What she saw in this
picture it is hard to say, as both the forest and the
buffalo had faded, the coyote was gone, and someone had punched holes in Adam Brady's eyes. But
whatever she saw, or thought she saw, she wrote to
him. In her letter, sealed with red wax, she enclosed
a picture of herself taken at a time when she had
been, almost, engaged. A touch of color had been
added to the cheeks. She gazed into a wicker cage
from which the happy bird had flown. We see her
facing this cage, her eyes on the empty perch, a
startled look of pleasure on her face, and though
she is plain, very plain, there is something about the
eyes—

> *I can see very clearly* [Adam Brady replied]
> *your lovely eyes, with the hidden smile, but I
> am not sure that I, nor any man, might plumb
> their depths and tell you what they mean. I fix
> my own eyes upon you without shame, and I
> see your face avert for my very boldness, and
> I can only compare the warm blush at your
> throat with the morning sky.*

Another place he spoke of the illicit sweetness
of the flesh.

—I can say I know the passions of the men about me, and the heated anguish of the blood, but I have never tasted the illicit sweetness of the flesh.

There was hardly room, in letters such as this, to speak of grasshopper plagues like swirling clouds in the sky, or of the wooden shapes of cattle frozen stiffly upright out on the range. No, it was hardly the place, and when she arrived, the last day of November, Adam Brady had to carry her through drifts of snow while leading his horse. There was no time for her to think, no place to reflect, there was nothing but the fact that a tall bearded man, smelling like a saddle blanket, carried her half a mile, then put her down on the ground *inside* of his house. There it was, right there beneath her, instead of a floor. Had there been something like a road, or a neighboring house, or a passing stranger that she might have called to, Will Jennings Brady, as we know him, might not have been born. But as it was, he came along soon enough. In September, when the grass had turned yellow on the sun-baked roof.

In this sod house, the cracked walls papered with calendar pictures of southern Indiana, Will jennings Brady, according to the record, was born. The grasshoppers ate the harness off a team of mares that year. That was how Adam Brady, his father, remembered it. Just four years later, in the month of October, Adam Brady put a roll of baling wire around his waist and went up the ladder on the windmill to make a repair. That was all that was known, and the story would have it that Emil Barton, the station agent, found him swinging like a bell clapper between the windmill posts. Adam Brady's boots were given to Emil Barton, as they still had, as was said, life in them, but his ticking watch was put aside for Will Brady, his son.

In the town of Indian Bow there was a dog named Shep, who was brown and white and had a long tail, and a boy named Gerald, about the same dirty color, but no tail. There was also a depot, a cattle loader, several square frame houses with clapboard privies; and later there were stores with pressed tin ceilings along the tracks. In the barber shop were a gum machine and a living rubber plant. Over this shop was a girl named Stella, who ate the boogers out of her nose, and her little brother Roger, who was inclined to eat everything else. Over the long dry summer it added up to quite a bit. But in Willy Brady's opinion it was still not enough.

From the roof of the soddy he could see the white valley road, the dry bed of the river, and the westbound freights slowly pulling up the grade. These trains might be there, winding up the valley, for an hour or more. Sometimes a gig or a tassel-fringed buggy that had left Indian Bow in the morning would still be there—that is, the dust would be there—in the afternoon. Like everything else, it didn't seem to know just where to go. The empty world in the valley seemed to be the only world there was. A boy on the roof of the soddy, or seated on the small drafty hole in the privy, might get the notion, now and then, that he was the last man in the world. That neither the freight trains, the buggy tracks, nor the dust was going anywhere. But if at times this empty world seemed unreal, or if he felt he was the last real man in it, he didn't let this feeling keep him awake at night, or warp his character. He grew up. He went to work for Emil Barton, the stationmaster.

Emil Barton passed most of the day near the stove where he could tip forward and spit in the wood-box, or open the stove door and make a quick fry-ing sound on the hot coals. Then he would twist his lips between his first finger and his thumb. That always left a brown stain on his thumb, and he would sit there, rubbing the stain between his fingers, and when it seemed to be gone he would hold these fingers to his nose. The smell never rubbed off. It always seemed to be there when he sniffed for it.

Will Brady remembered that, as he did the deep

10

scar on Emil Barton's forehead, which turned bluish white in winter as if the bone was showing through. It was said that this had happened over a woman, in a fight. It was said that Emil Barton had lost the woman, but the other man had lost his right eye, which Emil Barton kept in a whisky bottle at the back of his house.

As Emil Barton's assistant, Will Brady wore a cracked green visor with a soft leather band, black sateen dusters, and an indelible pencil behind one ear. During the long afternoons he sat at the window looking down the curving tracks to the semaphore, the switch near the cattle loader, and the bend in the river called Indian Bow. Now and then the Overland Express roared through, blowing on the windows like a winter gale, rocking the lamps in the station, and leaving a fine ashy grit on his teeth. Once or twice a year the express might stop, to pick up some cattleman or let one off, and when this happened the dining-car windows would throw their light on the tracks. Through the wide diner windows Will Brady would see the men and women from another world. They seemed to think Will Brady was as strange a sight as themselves. They would stare at him, he would stare at them, and then the train would take them off with just the blinking red lights, like a comet's tail, showing down the tracks.

Otherwise he might have stayed there, seated at the wide desk, listening to what the chirping ticker said, married Stella Bickel, and watered the rubber plant in her father's shop. But Stella Bickel married a brakeman on the C., B. & Q., and Indian Bow being on the Union Pacific, she moved east to Grand Island, where she could keep an eye on him. And just six months later, early in March, having made up her mind to go home to Indiana, Caroline Clayton Brady went to bed and died. The decision, Emil Barton said, was too much for her. He didn't say, in so many words, that it would soon be too much for Will Brady, but he let it be known that there were more things opening up down the line. East that is, down the grade toward Calloway. There was a roundhouse there, and a man could go to Omaha on week ends.

And Emil Barton was there, his hat in his hand, the sleeting rain cold on his bald head, when they stood on the raw pine board at the edge of his mother's grave. Over the wide valley spread a dim rain, the slopes of the hills grained like a privy clapboard, and the wind blowing a cloud of mist, like smoke, along the tracks. There was no woman at the station to see a man off—or ask him to hurry back. There was no dust to follow the dead wagon back into town. This desolate place, this rim of the world, had been God's country to Adam Brady, but to his wife, Caroline Clayton, a godforsaken hole. Perhaps only Will Brady could combine these two points of view. He could leave it, that is, but he would never get over it. *crippled because of it*

2

WHEN the eastbound freight pulled over on the siding, about half a mile west of the town of Calloway, Will Brady put on his shoes and came out on the platform of the caboose. Just north of the siding was a lumberyard where several men were working, piling new lumber, and beyond the yard was a long frame building with a flat roof. Eight or ten young women were out on the roof, drying their hair. When they saw Will Brady two of the girls jeered at him. They were very young, with loud voices, and this may have had something to do with the fact that Will Brady took a great interest in the lumberyard. One of the men in the yard wore a carpenter's apron, with deep nail pockets at the front, but another seemed to carry all the nails he needed in his mouth. He fed them out, one at a time, as he hammered them.

Now, these goings on seemed to interest Will Brady very much. He had never seen so much wood before—perhaps that was it. Nor so many women—though he preferred one woman at a time. And there was one, oddly enough, seated on the porch. This woman had also washed her hair, and one man might have judged it golden, like corn silk, while another might have found it somewhat brittle, more the color of straw. But there it was, anyhow, drying on her head. She wore a green kimono with faded red dragons on the loose sleeves. In her hand she held a magazine, but so great was her interest in the lumberyard, and in what the men were doing, that it was placed face-down in her lap. When the men dropped the timber she watched the yellow sawdust rise in the air. She saw it collect in the dark beard of the man who ran the saw. Perhaps it was the smell, like one out of a garden, or the noon sun beating down on the yellow timber, or the white arms of the men now that it was spring and their sleeves were rolled, but whatever it was, it seemed to her a marvelous sight. Not once did she raise her eyes to the young man in the wide-brimmed hat, his face in shadow, standing on the platform of the caboose. Would that explain what came over him? Why, as the express roared past, he took the wide-brimmed hat from his head and sailed it out on the air, as if the wind had sucked it off? There it sailed through the air, the woman looking at it, and as the freight began to move, the young man threw his wicker bag into the ditch, jumped after it. After all, that had been his father's hat. There would be another train, but perhaps in all the world just one hat like that. So he went after the hat, and it would be hard to say whether the woman with the yellow hair saw or did not see what a fine young man he was. A little narrow in the shoulders, but with his father's long legs. And now that his hat was off, there was his mother's wavy hair. Whether she saw these things or not there is no telling, as his hat was on, his face was in shadow, when he walked past her toward the town. No telling what she thought, but every indication that she sized him up.

Through the window of the Merchant's Hotel he could see the potted palms at the front of the lobby, and the row of oak rockers, with leather seats, facing the tracks. In one of the rockers sat a man with a black linen vest. He wore elastic bands on his sleeves, and in one pocket of the linen vest were several indelible pencils with bright red caps. The man was large, but he didn't look too well. His face was about the same color as his light tan button shoes, and when he got out of the rocker he took his time, as if he needed help. But he was friendly enough. As they walked back to the desk he rested one hand on Will Brady's shoulder and with the other slipped a chew of tobacco into his mouth.

"Young man," he said, "I take it you missed your train?"

"I got off," Will Brady said, "I was getting off."

"My name is Bassett," the big man said, "two esses and two tees." He smiled, then he said: "There's nothing in Omaha we haven't got right here." He let that sink in, then he said: "You know what I mean?" Will Brady nodded his head. The man laughed, then went on: "Hotel on the European plan, girls on the American plan—you know what I mean?"

"Yes sir," said Will Brady, as his mother had brought him up right.

"Young man," said Mr. Bassett, and took from the case a box of cigars, placed it on the counter, "I could use a man like you right here if he wasn't afraid of work." He let that sink in, then he said: "Have a cigar?"

"No, thank you, sir," Will Brady said, "I don't smoke."

"You don't smoke?" said Mr. Bassett.

"I just never started," said Will Brady.

"You like a drink?" said Mr. Bassett.

"Thank you very much," Will Brady said, "but I don't drink."

"What is your name, son?" Mr. Bassett said, and put his hands on the counter as if for support. His mouth stood open, and Will Brady saw the purple pencil stain on his lip.

"Brady, sir," he said, "Will Jennings Brady."

"You don't drink an' you don't smoke," Mr. Bassett said. "Tell me, boy—you anything against the ladies?"

"No, sir," said Will Brady, and took off his hat as his face felt hot. From the pocket of his coat he took a clean handkerchief and blew his nose into it.

3

As the night clerk in the Merchant's Hotel, Will Brady wore a green visor, quite a bit like the old one, and a vest that Mr. Bassett ordered for him from Omaha. There were pockets in the vest for indelible pencils, a new stem-wind Dueber-Hampden, and the cigars that traveling men might offer him. "Just because you don't smoke, son," Mr. Bassett had said, "don't think you're any better than the man who does." By that he meant to accept the cigar and keep his mouth shut. Give it back to the man the next time he came around. In the last pocket, pinned there, was the key to the coin drawer. In the coin drawer were stamps, fifty dollars in silver, and a Colt revolver with five deep notches in the mother-of-pearl handle. During the night the Colt was slung in the holster strapped to the leg of the desk.

Most of the day Will Brady slept in a room with several copper fire extinguishers, a stack of galvanized buckets, and about sixty feet of cracked canvas hose. A good many traveling men fell asleep while smoking their cigars. Others were apt to doze off in the lobby, a coat pocket or a vest burning, and the smell in some cases was not much different from that of the cigar. He would have to leave the desk and walk up front for a look at them. On the back of each room door he nailed a sign bearing the signature of Ralph O. Bassett:

PUT OUT CIGAR
Before
PUTTING OUT LIGHTS

Twelve hours a night he sat in the lobby facing the map of the state of Nebraska, or the Seth Thomas clock which he wound once a week. On the wall with the clock were five or six railroad calendars. A man with time on his hands might imagine himself in the Royal Gorge, crossing the Great Divide, or with the honeymoon couple as they motored through the Garden of the Gods. There were no pictures of Indiana, nor of holy men feeding the birds, but, thanks to his mother, he was at home with calendars. They were alike, in that the scenes were all far away.

Nearer at home was the map of Nebraska, with the chicken-track railroad lines, and the dark-ringed holes that the traveling men had burned with their cigars. One at Calloway, Grand Island, Columbus, and Omaha. Every now and then a town was added, the name printed in by the man who had found it, with the help of other men who had been there or had some notion where it was. The country was booming, as one man said. This man could prove it to you, pointing at the map, but the truth was that Will Brady, who seemed bright enough in some ways, had a hard time visualizing such things. He could stare for hours at the hole in the map without seeing very much. Eyes open, all he saw was the map; and eyes closed, all that came to mind was the smell of the floor mop and the ticking of the Seth Thomas clock.

He had arranged with Ralph Bassett to take the night off once a week. What was there to do with it in a place like Calloway? A married man, of course, didn't face the same problem, but when Will Brady took the night off he walked down the tracks to the building where the girls washed their hair on the roof. At the side of this building was a sagging flight of stairs with a lantern at the top. If this lantern happened to be burning, it was Will Brady's night off. The wire handle on the lantern would be hot from the flame, and he would have to wrap his handkerchief around it before he took it down from the hook and opened the door. With the smoking lantern in his hand, he would step inside. He had learned to set it on the floor, not the rug, but he had still not learned how to take off his shoes, or his socks, without sitting down on the side of the bed. He would tap the cinders in the heels of his shoes into the palm of his hand. If it was summer and warm, he might even take off his socks.

What was he up to? Well, the woman in the bed had a word for it. He was a lover. That was her way of putting it. Her name was Opal Mason and she talked pretty frankly about some things. That might seem an odd way to describe a man who brought nothing along, said nothing loving, and left a good deal up to the woman, to say the least. A lover in some ways perhaps, but not too bright. He went about his business and then he rolled over and went to sleep.

He also slept very well, while she seemed to sleep indifferently; sleeping was something she could do, as she put it, at another time. It was not something she did when she had other things on her mind. The lover lay on his side, his heavy head on her arm, his breath blowing wisps of yellow hair in her face, and she lay on her back listening to the engines switch around in the yard. A big woman, with straw-colored hair, Opal Mason usually cried when somebody died, when babies were born, or when certain men slept with her. Like the lover, for instance. Something about it struck her as sad. In her opinion, a woman's opinion, there was something very lonely about a lantern, the tooting of switch engines, and the way men were inclined to fall asleep. Something strange, that is, about lying awake with a man sound asleep. Perhaps this struck her as the loneliest thing of all. The town of Calloway struck her as lonely since she had the smoking lanterns, the tooting engines, and the sleeping lover all at one time. It made her strangely melancholy. It was a pleasure for her to cry.

Every lover took time as well as patience; and lying awake, Opal Mason had come to have the notion that men did not come, the lovers did not come, merely to sleep with her. No, they came into the room, the lantern in their hand, for something else. In her opinion, all of these strong silent men were scared to death. Of what? Perhaps they were scared of themselves. They were all such strong, silent men, and they all seemed to think they would live forever, make love forever, and then drop off to sleep as they always did. They were like children, and if they came to her—more, that is, than to the younger women—perhaps she reminded them of what the situation really was. There were all sorts of men, of course, there were those who seemed to know this and those who didn't, and then there was this lover, Will Brady, who didn't seem to know anything. That might be what she liked about him. Lying awake she often wondered if that was what he liked about her.

"You men!" she would say, wagging her head, and as this sometimes woke him up, he would rise on his elbow and ask her what the trouble was. For all that, she never seemed to know. She would tell him to please shut up and go back to sleep. From the pocket of the green kimono that she wore she would take the package of Sen-Sen, put some in her mouth, and then lie there whiffling through her nose and sucking on it. It was not the kind of thing a man like Will Brady could appreciate. If the weather was bad, or the room was cold, he would lie there and try to ignore it, but on the warm summer nights he would get up and put on his shoes. On his way out he would blow out the lantern before he hung it back on the wall, and if the night was clear he might remember to look at his watch. He didn't like to get caught along the tracks when number 9 went through, at three in the morning, so he might stand there till he heard the whistle far down the line. He would still be there, later, watching the receding lights on the caboose.

Sen-Sen, of course, was a small matter, but there was nothing small about her old friends, several dozens of them, who might pop up at any time. Men from as far away as Salt Lake City and Cheyenne. Busy men who found the time, somehow or other, to stop off. And from June through September, four pretty long months, Opal Mason met all of her old friends in Denver, where she liked the climate better, as she said, for a woman in her work. Also, why did she have to mention it? These things were not small, they were serious, and they had led better men than himself to see the weakness in the American plan. It wasn't women he wanted—what he wanted was a woman for himself.

Ralph Bassett, for example, had one, and Will Brady saw quite a bit of her as she spent most of the day on the wire-legged stool in the Hotel Café. She kept Ralph Bassett's books, and once a week typed out a new menu. As there wasn't too much for her to do she spent a good deal of time peering into the pie case, where there was a mirror, and adjusting the hairpins in her heavy black hair. With her arms raised, the bone pins in her mouth, she would arch her broad back and turn on the stool to look at her face, and her hair, in the pie case. Part of Will Brady's trouble over the summer was certainly due to the fact that the long summer days, and the heat, were hard on Ethel Bassett's hair. She spent a good deal of time with her arms raised, fixing it. On the wall behind her was a mirror, so that Will Brady saw her both front and back, in the round so to speak, while she looked him straight in the face. Which was odd, as she never seemed to see anything. A wall might as well have been there, but none was. Ethel Bassett had large dark eyes, and a face that any man would call handsome, but it would be hard to say what she had on her mind. The phases of the moon? Well, she sometimes spoke of that. He had once seen a book with pictures of the stars open in her lap. There was also her son, a boy named Orville, who liked to hug his mother most of the time, and there was some indication, Will Brady thought, that she egged him on. Anyhow, it didn't help a young man settle his mind. Over a long hot summer, while Opal Mason was cooling in Denver, he had nothing to do but watch Ethel Bassett put up her long black hair.

Suitable women, as Ralph Bassett liked to say, were pretty damn scarce. They were safe at home in one of the tree-shaded houses some man like Ralph Bassett had built for them, or they wore sunbonnets and walked about among the flowers with watering cans. Or they were very young, their hair in long braids as in the album pictures of his mother, or they were too old, peering at him over a line of wash, clothespins in their mouths and another woman's baby at their feet. He saw the arms of these women, from time to time, drooping from some hammock like a strand of rope, and other times he heard them at the back of a lawn, in a creaking lawn swing. Their age was uncertain, but it was known they were spoken for. They were as near and as far as the women he saw in the dining cars.

"And now what is it?" Opal Mason would say, as she couldn't stand a man thinking. A man lying *there* and thinking, that is.

"Can't a man just lie here?" he would say.

"You're not just lying there—you're thinking!" she'd say, and there was no use asking such a woman what was wrong with that. He could lie somewhere else, she would tell him, if he wanted to think. But he didn't. It was just that he thought while lying there with her. Trying to think what a suitable woman would be like.

For the important thing about Opal Mason, a "very unsuitable woman," was that he knew what he knew, and she knew, and that suited him. The only unsuitable thing was some ten or twenty other men. The only way to settle a thing like that was to make her a suitable woman, to buy a ring with a stone and make this woman his wife. With the summer coming on he made up his mind, ordered a ring with a stone from a house in Grand Island, and near the middle of May, a warm spring night, he shaved and rinsed with bay rum. He wore the vest to his suit so that he could take the ring along. He walked down the tracks, on the ties this time, to keep the cinders out of his shoes, and with the smoking lantern he stepped into the room, softly closed the door. For reasons of her own, Opal Mason was awake, playing solitaire. Not many women look good sitting up in bed, whether they're playing solitaire or not, and the idea crossed his mind that maybe the time was not right. But he had waited too long, and what he had come to say came out. Still holding the lantern, he said: "Opal—I want you for my wife."

It was some time before she said anything. Before she moved, or anything like a thought crossed her broad face. In that amount of time he saw the board in her lap, a packing-case board with the name RORTY on it, and fanned out on the board her very soiled deck of cards. At the moment he spoke, her right hand had been raised, the thumb ready to flick the tip of her tongue, and the tip of that thumb was white as a blister, the dirt licked off. He saw all of that, then he realized that where he hurt —for he hurt somewhere—was the wire handle of the lantern burning his right hand. "Ouch," he said, but not so much in pain as in what you might call recognition. Then he bent over to lower the lantern to the floor. He was still bent over when he heard Opal Mason begin to laugh.

Now, the thing is that Opal Mason never laughed. In order to account for what he did later you have to keep in mind that Opal Mason, a big sad-eyed woman, often cried a good deal but she never laughed. She grinned now and then, but nearly always covered her mouth, as if her teeth hurt her if she felt a smile on it. A laugh was such an odd sound, coming from her, that the man with the lantern doubted his senses, bending nearer as if to make sure for himself. But the woman was laughing, there was no doubt of it. Perhaps it was the *ouch* that struck her as funny, coming right at the time it did, rather than the sober, simple statement she had heard. Perhaps. Or the fact that he didn't find it funny himself. There's a pretty good chance that if he had laughed she would have married him. But he was an odd one, no doubt about that, and while Opal Mason laughed herself sick he picked up his lantern and went out on the porch. He hung it back on the hook and made his way to the foot of the stairs. There he found a light in the front hall as it was still early, around midnight, and four or five girls had come out on the porch to see what was wrong. Nobody had ever heard Opal Mason laugh before. To these girls, standing there together, one of them in a shawl she had wrapped around her, Will Brady said: "Is there one of you girls that would like to get married?" That did it. They began to laugh, they saw the joke. "I'm not joking," Will Brady said. "Is there one of you girls that would like to get married?"

One girl stopped laughing and said: "Mickey. I guess Mickey would."

"Who is Mickey?" he said, and stepped up on the porch. He was shy of young girls who were bold and named everything freely, but right at the moment he was not shy. He was bold himself. "Where is Mickey?" he said, and for some reason took off his hat.

"My God!" said one girl. "Go get him Mickey!" and they held on to him, holding his arms, while they ran down the long hall to the rear, then came running back. "Here's Mickey," they said, and brought the girl out. She was a kid, maybe fifteen, sixteen years old. She was a thin, flat girl with her hair in braids looped up like stirrups, and there were scratched mosquito bites on her arms and skinny legs. A girl not so thin wouldn't have looked so pregnant, so swelled up.

"I understand you would like a good man," he said, in a friendly way, and smiling at her, but this kid stepped forward and slapped him full in the face. It left his cheek numb, and one eye seeing double, but she stood right before him, her fists clenched, and in the quiet he could hear her gritting her small pointed teeth. He just looked at her, he didn't raise his hand and give her a cuff. After all, just an hour before, he had shaved himself, rinsed with sweet-smelling water, and come down the tracks to ask a woman to be his wife. In the right-hand pocket of his vest was a ring, with an eighty-dollar stone. It makes a difference, something like that, and perhaps even this kid felt it as her teeth stopped gritting and she began to snuffle through her nose. She didn't want to let on that she had started to bawl. There were freckles straddling her nose, and tangled in with her braids were strips of colored ribbon, but looking at her Will Brady didn't feel very much. He was thinking of himself, and what he was doing, and what a fine thing it was for a man like himself to behave so well with a kid like that. No, he didn't feel much of anything till she slapped him again. With her left hand, across the other side of his face. You have to give it to a kid like that, a kid with that kind of spunk. Until that occurred you might even say that Will Brady hadn't really thought about her, but as a boy he had always taken his hat off to spunk. He didn't have a whole lot of it, put it like that. Before she slapped him again—and he saw it coming—he bent over and scooped her off her feet, and she beat on his head with her fists doubled up, smashing down his hat. Then she suddenly stopped, hugged him tight, and began to bawl.

He carried her down from the porch and along the fence that went around the sawmill, down through the ditch, then up the steep gravel bank to the tracks. He walked on the ties toward the red and green lights in the semaphore. Although she was a skinny girl, she was a little heavier than she ought to be, and not the right shape for carrying more than a quarter mile. Near the water tank he had to stop and put her down. His arms were asleep, his hands were prickly, and he stood there holding her hand and listening to the waterspout drip on the tracks.

"How much further are we going?" she said.

He hadn't thought. He hadn't thought about that part of it.

"Before we go any further," she said, "I think I better tell you we can't get married."

"We can't?"

"I'm already married," she said. "I'm as good as married, that is."

As he was still holding her hand he put it down and said: "I've got a ring here—now why don't you use it?" He took the ring from the pocket in his vest, put it in her hand. "As I won't need it now, you use it," he said. There was a moon behind her, and she turned so that the light fell on the stone.

"Is that the real McCoy?" she said.

"That's the real McCoy," he said. She closed her hand on it and put that hand behind her back.

"What's your name?"

"Brady," he said, "Will Brady."

"My name is Mickey Ahearn right now," she said.

"I'm down here in the hotel," he said, and pointed down the tracks past the semaphore. "The Merchant's Hotel. I'm in the lobby most of the time."

"I'll remember," she said, "I always remember everything."

"Well," he said, rubbing his hands, "it's getting pretty cool, you better run along." She ran off like a kid for about thirty yards, then she stopped. She stood there between the tracks, looking back at him. "You shouldn't run like that any more," he said. "You're not a kid any more, you're a lady."

"That's what I just remembered."

"Well, now you go along," he said. He turned and walked a little ways himself, but when he turned back she was still there. "Now you go along," he said, and shooed his hand at her, like a friendly dog, but she didn't move, so he turned and walked away. When he looked back from the station platform, she was gone.

4

I N   N O V E M B E R Will Brady was sitting in the lobby, waiting for the local to come down from North Platte, when he saw Mickey Ahearn on the platform of the eastbound caboose. She was standing there, her hands on the brake wheel, beside a boy by the name of Popkov, one of the section hands on the C., B. & Q. One of those foreign kids with curly hair that seemed to grow right out of his eyes. He had one hand on her arm, and with the other he held a large duffel bag. Mickey Ahearn looked straight down the tracks toward the sawmill until the caboose passed the hotel, when she turned her head sharply as if she had thought of him. But the sun was on the window, and besides he was behind a potted plant. This kid Popkov might have seen him but there was no reason for him to look, and he kept his eyes, like those of a bird, right down the tracks. So did Will Brady, until the eastbound freight had pulled out of sight.

* * *

In the Wilderness

Early in the spring, about the first week of March, Fred Blake, the Calloway station agent, called Will Brady up and said that he would like to speak to him. "Right away, Brady," he said. "Got something over here with your name on it."

That was a Sunday morning, the one he liked to sleep, but Will Brady got out of bed as it wasn't often anybody sent him anything. As he crossed the tracks he could see that Mrs. Blake, a big, motherly woman, was sitting there in the office with a wicker basket in her lap. The basket was covered with a cloth, like a lunch, but a red American Express tag, fastened on with a wire, dangled from the handle on one end.

As he opened the door Will Brady said: "Somebody put me up a good picnic lunch?" as Fred Blake himself was quite a kidder and liked a good joke.

"This ain't exactly a picnic," Fred Blake said, and though it was too early for flies in the office, he waved his hand over the basket as if there were. Then he raised one corner of the towel, peeked in. "No, this ain't no picnic, Will," he said, and still holding the corner of the towel, he stepped aside so Will Brady could see for himself. No, it was no picnic. A sausage-colored baby lay asleep on its face. A soiled nightshirt, or whatever it is that babies wear that leave their bottoms uncovered, was in a wadded roll around its neck. On the baby's left leg, tied there with a string, was another American Express tag, and Will Brady turned this one over to see what it said.

My name is Willy Brady

and that was all.

"It's a boy?" Will Brady said.

"He's a boy," said Mrs. Blake, and rolled him over on his back, and he was a boy, all right. Around his neck was a strand of black hair with a gold ring braided to it. The ring had what looked to be about an eighty-dollar stone.

"How old you reckon he is, Mrs. Blake?" he said.

"He's about five weeks," Mrs. Blake said, and then she put the knuckle of her little finger in the boy's mouth. She let him suck on it for a bit, then she took it out, sniffed the knuckle, and said: "The poor little tyke—a bottle baby." She shook her head sadly, put the knuckle back again.

"There's an orphanage in Kearney," Fred Blake said. "Think they call it Sister something or other. They say it's not a bad place, don't they, Kate?"

"It's not bad," she said, "as them places go."

"Unless you was thinking," Fred Blake said, "of something yourself."

Had Will Brady been thinking? No. But now he would.

"If it was a girl," Mrs. Blake said, "now I wouldn't know what to think. But there's nearly always someone, it seems to me, who wants a fine boy."

"Don't get in a hurry now, Kate," said Fred. "After all, this boy's got Will's name on him. Maybe Will here would like a husky boy himself."

Mrs. Blake smelled the knuckle of her little finger again. "The poor little tyke," she said, "the poor little tyke."

"Mrs. Blake," Will Brady said, "what would you say he'd need besides a good bottle?"

Mrs. Blake opened her mouth, wide, then she seemed to change her mind.

"What'd you say he'd need, Kate?" said Fred.

"He could use a good woman," Kate Blake said, and scooped the baby up. "You mind I take him home and feed him, Will?" she said.

"Why, no," Will Brady said.

"Kate," Fred Blake said, "what do you say we just keep him till Will here picks up what he needs?"

"Won't that take him some time?" Kate Blake said, and they stood there, looking at her. "You men!" she said, and with the boy hugged tight she went through the door. Then she put her head back in and said: "Now I'll tell you when to come around. I don't want you, either of you, moping around the house." With that she let the door slam, and through the wide window they watched her cross the tracks.

"That's the way they get," Fred Blake said. "Just let a kid come along and that's the way they get." He turned to the basket and said: "What'll we do with this—you won't be needing it."

This Willy Brady was an odd one for a boy, as he wasn't much bigger than a rabbit, and he had the dark unblinking eyes of a bird. They were neither friendly nor unfriendly, nor were they blue like Will Brady's, the watery blue of the faded summer sky. They were more like the knobs on a hatpin than eyes. They seemed to pick up, Will Brady thought, right where his mother's eyes had left off, staring at him from the top step of the porch.

It also seemed to be clear that somebody had made a mistake. If Will Brady had fathered this boy—as Fred Blake liked to say—then Prince Albert was the son of Daniel Boone. The little fellow was also, as Mrs. Blake said, pretty bright. He seemed to have taken after his mother in most respects.

If Will Brady took exception to this he never

let on, nor troubled to deny it, but just went about the business of being a father to the boy. That is to say that once or twice a week he bounced the boy on his knee in a horsey manner, and let him play with the elastic arm bands on his sleeves. Mrs. Blake referred to him as Daddy, to herself as Grandma, but she might call the boy any number of things. Sometimes she called him Cookie because of his black currant eyes.

"Now give Cookie to his grandma," she would say, and swing the boy in the air by his heels; but let Will Brady try that and there would be hell to pay. The boy would scrounge around, grunt like a pig, or hold his breath till his black eyes popped. He would turn a grape color and scare Will Brady half to death. "Here, give him to his granny," she would say, and of course he would.

Other times the boy would just sit in his lap like a big cat, watching his face, and making Will Brady so self-conscious he couldn't move his lips. He never said a word about it, naturally, but he knew long before the boy had said a word, any more than da-da, that talking was going to be something of a problem for both of them. Fred Blake could make a fine assortment of faces, barnyard noises, and the like, but as for Will Brady he couldn't even whistle properly. Nor was the one face he had strictly his own. He knew that whenever the boy stared at

37

him. It was just something that he wore that people like the boy saw right through. About all that he could do was wear arm bands with bright metal clips, or gay ribbons, wind his watch with the key, and keep penny candy in the pockets of his vest. Once a month he would bring the boy something special from Omaha. Something he could eat, ride, put together, or take apart.

Will Brady went to Omaha with the idea that almost any day, any warm Sunday morning, he might find Mickey Ahearn out walking on Douglas Street. He might see her in one of the doorways, or leaning out of one of the upstairs windows, with that boy Popkov, or somebody just like him, right at her back. He would be a foreigner, and the hair would be growing right out of his eyes. He also looked in jewelry stores, or better-class pawnshops, thinking he might find her choosing a ring, one with a stone that would be the real McCoy. All he wanted to do was to tell her what a fine healthy boy she had, but that it wouldn't hurt him any if he had his own mother one of these days. That was all. He wasn't going to force anything on her. In his wallet he had a picture of the boy seated on a wire chair, like those they have in drugstores, holding a wicker bird-cage and a Bible in his lap. The boy's mouth was open and you could see his three front teeth.

He would find her and show her this picture, and while she looked at the picture he would study her face, trying to make up his mind if she would be a good mother or not. If he thought she would, he would repeat what he once said. Let bygones be bygones, he would say. If she didn't look healthy, or didn't seem to care, or if she was still married to this Popkov—if that was how it was, why then he would have to think of something else.

He didn't have to think, as it turned out, very long. He never saw nor heard of Mickey Ahearn again, but the spring the boy was three years old, by Mrs. Blake's reckoning, he brought him a birthday present from Omaha. An Irish Mail, with a bright red seat—one of the many things the boy would have to grow into—Will Brady brought it back with him on the train. As he got off, down the tracks from the station, he saw a large funeral passing through town, and he stood there wondering whose funeral it was. In the lead buggy was Reverend Wadlow, and there at his side, wrapped up in a robe, was the widow—a woman who didn't look any too old. She was dressed in black, with a veil, and as the buggy rocked on the tracks she lifted this veil, deliberately, and looked at him. The same kind of look, whatever it was, that Ethel Bassett usually gave him in the pie-case mirror, she now gave him directly, then lowered the veil. In the buggy behind her was her son Orville, with members of her family, who were said to be Bohemians, and who had driven down from their farm near Bruno to be with her. Will Brady stood there, watching, until Fred Blake came along and picked him up.

That same evening, driving the team that Ralph Bassett reserved for Sundays, he drove the widow to the evening service at the church. From there he drove her home, put the team in the barn, and seeing that the spring grass needed cutting, he came back the following day and cut it for her. It was no more than Ralph Bassett's widow had the right to expect. She brought him a cool glass of grape juice, and while he stood there in the yard, sipping it, she sat in the chain swing behind the wire baskets of ferns.

The place needed a man, she said—needed a man to keep it up.

He agreed with that, and when he finished with the grape juice he said that the place needed a man, the way a man with a boy needed a home.

He didn't wait to see if she agreed with that or not. He put the glass on the porch and walked the mower through the grass to the back of the house.

5

THE HOUSE Ralph Bassett had built for his wife was full of furniture made in Grand Rapids, and in the gables were diamond-shaped pieces of colored glass. When the sun shone through the glass it reminded a railroad man, like Will Brady, of the red and green lights in the semaphores. Inside of the house, it was one of the things that made him at home. In the summer these colors might be on the floor, or cast on the goldfish bowl near the table, but in the winter they made a bright pattern on the wall. Or on the man who now sat at the head of the table, whoever he was. The food on the table was sometimes red, but the man at the table was usually green owing to the way he liked to lean forward, his head cocked to the side. The green light could be seen on his forehead, his wavy dark hair. Out of habit, perhaps, Will Brady—the man who now sat at the head of the table—liked to cock his head and keep one eye on the green light. That was what he liked to see down the spur of tracks, where the switch was open, and in the brakeman's lantern at the top of Opal Mason's stairs. Green. There was something friendly about it.

When the green light was not on his face Will

Brady might see, through the rippling bay window, the shrubs that were cut to look like giant birds, or little girls holding hands. Men who thought the house looked like a caboose might not see them curtsy in the wind, or the rambling rose vine that crawled up their arms to put flowers in their hair. But on Sunday, beyond the arbor, any man with eyes could see the tasseled buggies that scoffers drove by, very slowly, to see the house for themselves. Or to remark that Will Brady, seated in the chain swing, or mowing the lawn, had the look of a man who felt at home about the place.

Another man might smoke, or take it easy, but getting up from the table Will Brady would say: "Well, this isn't getting the grass cut," and hang his coat and vest on the back of his chair. He was not much of a hand with shrubs, but he could mow a lawn. As it happened to be quite a piece of lawn, maybe half an acre if you counted in the barn, by the time he was through in the back it was long in the front again. Not that he minded. Maybe he needed the exercise. As a matter of fact he liked a big lawn, with a few big shady elms around it, and a house with a swing and a wire basket of ferns on the front porch. He had a taste for the good things. Maybe it came natural to him.

When Ethel Bassett had to go and visit her people he slept in the house, in the guest room, as she felt better with a man in the house, as she said. Her maiden name was Czerny, and this helped to explain some of the things he felt about her, as foreigners were apt to be different in funny ways. When her father drove over for her he first spoke of his horses, wanting feed and water for them, then he spoke of his family, the weather, or whatever might come to mind. Ethel Bassett would go home with him, over Sunday, helping her mother with the Sunday meal, and then visiting the cemetery, where the stones were marked with foreign names. Some of them like her own, others hardly pronounceable. Ethel Bassett's feelings about these things was what Will Brady would call religious, as distinct from what he was apt to feel himself. He liked it. It was a thing to respect in her. There was something there, something to go back to, that he didn't seem to have, and he saw that it gave her an advantage over himself. It was part of the finer things she had around the house. It was his own suggestion that he stay in the house—look after these things, as he put it—so she wouldn't have something like that on her mind.

He slept in the guest room, which was on the south side of the house, facing the tracks, but a different air seemed to blow in the window from that in the hotel. It smelled of the grass he had cut himself. The bed seemed to be softer, and even his sleep seemed sounder, though he was a sound enough sleeper, normally. Something about the idea of a place of his own. The keys in his pocket to the cellar door, the lock on the barn. In the morning he served himself a good breakfast, eating his bacon and eggs in the kitchen, but putting off the coffee until he stood in the dining-room. Later he would walk from room to room, his feet quiet on the Axminster rugs.

No, it doesn't take long to get used to the finer things. All you need are the things, and a man with the taste for them. A woman with bird's-eye maple in her room, and small cut-glass bottles, with large stoppers, and an ivory box with long strands of her combed-out hair. Dark and soft as corn silk, not at all wiry like her red-haired boy. Somehow, he didn't care for the boy—his own boy struck him as a good deal finer, and the only thing in Calloway that went with the house. An imported look, like the glass chimes on the front porch. But there was nothing wrong with Ethel Bassett, nothing that he could see. A quiet woman, not given to talk, with something of a religious nature, she seemed to rely on him now that Ralph Bassett was gone. She left it up to him to shovel the snow from in front of the house. And when the snow was gone, it was up to him to cut the grass. He used a grass-catcher on the mower, but when the grass was damp, or he walked

a little fast, it would miss the catcher entirely and
stick to his pants, so he would need a broom from
the kitchen to sweep himself off, and if it was summer he would need a cooling drink—grape juice,
with a lump of ice in it, or fresh lemonade. And
after putting away the mower he would walk
around to the side of house where there was a
faucet, and rinse off his hands. It was her own suggestion that he do that in the house. One thing like
that leads to another, so he got in the habit of using
the kitchen, and she got in the habit of standing
there with him, holding the towel. Now, he didn't
need a towel—that was what he always said. But
she would wag her head, as women do when they
find something like that in a man, and he would take
the towel but only use the corner of it. And when
he rolled down his sleeves, she would hold his coat
for him. That was all. There was no need to say
anything. Perhaps this was why the night that she
spoke he was not at all sure that he had heard her,
or that she had said what he thought he had heard.

"Yes—?" he said, and stood there, holding his
hat.

What did he think of all the talk, she had said. So
he had heard it all right. That was what she had
said.

"Talk?" he said. "What talk?" and put his right
hand into his pocket, as he did when the boy put a

hard question to him. With the boy all he had to do was give him something.

There was talk of their getting married, she said, and he stood there, his hand in his pocket, then he took the hand out and looked at the rusty tenpenny nail. He used the nail to clean his thumbnail, then he said that if there was talk of that kind, he hadn't heard it, but if he had heard it he wouldn't have done much of anything. What he meant to say was that talk like that didn't bother him. That was what he said, then he put the head of the tenpenny nail in his mouth and saw that she was looking at him as she did in the pie case, her eyes wide. He saw that this blank expression, this look she gave him, was meant to be an open one. He was meant to look in, and he tried, but he didn't see anything.

There was talk of their getting married, she repeated, so he raised his voice and said that if that was the talk, why he had no objection. That was all right with him. If that was the talk, he said, his voice ringing, why, let them talk.

Would he be able to wait, she said, another three months?

Would he be able? Why, yes. He nodded his head. Yes, he repeated, he would be able to wait three months. Then he followed her out on the porch, full of wonder about what he had been saying, and picked up the paper, the Omaha Sunday paper, he had left on the swing. He put his paper in his pocket, then he took it out and waved to a man in a passing buggy, then he went down the seven steps and crossed the lawn. There was a brick sidewalk, but he stepped across it, waded into the road. From the park across the street a boy ran out, circled him twice, then ran off crying:

> *Strawberry shortcake,*
> *Huckleberry Pie,*
> *Pee in the road*
> *An' you'll get a sty.*

Somehow it made him feel better, and without looking back he walked off through the park.

IN THE CLEARING

1

THEY WERE married in Bruno, a Bohemian town in the rolling country just south of the Platte, four or five miles' drive from where her father had a big farm. They were married in the church where Ralph Bassett had married her. It sat on the rise, overlooking the town, and as it was June the door stood open and Will Brady could see the buggies drawn up beneath the shade trees out in front. An elderly man was combing sandburs from a dark mare's tail. It was quiet on the rise, without a leaf stirring, but in the sunny hollow along the tracks a westerly breeze was turning the wheel of a giant windmill. It looked softly blurred, quite a bit the way the heat made everything look in Indian Bow, with the air, like a clear stream of water, flowing up from the hot earth. Near the windmill a man was sinking a post, and the sound of the blows, like jug corks popping, came up in the pause that his mallet hung in the air. Fred Blake had to remind him—nudging him sharply—to kiss the bride.

They went to Colorado Springs, where he sat in the lobby, reading the latest Denver papers, and giving her time, as he said to himself, to compose herself. A little after ten o'clock he went up, and as he opened the door he saw her, seated at her dressing-table, her face in the mirror. The eyes were wide and blank, just as they were in the pie case. She did not smile, nor make any sign that she recognized him. Could he bring her something, he asked, but when she neither moved nor seemed to hear him, he closed the door and walked to the end of the hall. There was a balcony there, facing the mountains, and maybe he stood there for some time, for when he came back to the room, the lights were off. He did not turn them on, but quietly undressed in the dark.

As he had never been married before, or spent a night in bed with a married woman, there were many things, perhaps, that he didn't know much about. That was why he was able to lie there, all night, and think about it. The woman beside him, his wife, was rolled up tight in the sheet. She had used the sheet on top for this purpose so that he was lying next to the blanket, a woolly one, and perhaps that helped keep him awake. She seemed to be wrapped from head to foot, as mummies are wrapped. It occurred to him that something like that takes a good deal of practice, just as it took practice to lie, wrapped up like a mummy, all night. It took practice, and it also took something else. It took fear. This woman he had married was scared to death.

When a person is scared that bad, what can you do? You can lie awake, for one thing, in case this person might be lonely, or, like Opal Mason, in case she didn't like men who fell asleep. But it was hard to picture Opal Mason rolled up in a sheet. Or what it was now in this room that frightened this woman. As he had never been married before, he was not as upset as he might have been, for it occurred to him that there might be something he hadn't been told. In the marriage of widows, perhaps, a ceremony. A ritual that called for spending one night rolled up in a sheet. He had heard of such things. It was something he could think about. There was also the fact that this woman was a Bohemian, a foreigner, and perhaps she had foreign ways. But nobody had told him. And while he wondered, she fell asleep.

In time he fell asleep himself, but not too well beneath the woolly blanket, which may have been why he dreamed as he did, and remembered it. He saw before him Ralph Bassett, standing behind the desk. He had a large paunch, larger than he remembered, and the front of his vest, between the lower buttons, was worn threadbare where he rubbed against the handle of the coin drawer. A strange dream, but Will Brady fathomed it. All these years —and it seemed very long—Ralph Bassett had rubbed the coin drawer during the day, then he had gone home to rub against his mummy-wrapped wife at night. It didn't strike him as funny. Nor did it strike him as out of this world. If a woman has lived twelve years with a man, and the nights of those years rolled up in a sheet, and this woman was now your wife, it deserved serious thought. And while he thought, this woman, his wife, snored heavily.

Their honeymoon room had a view of the mountains, with Pike's Peak, and a cloud of snow on it, and as it was warm these windows were open on the sky. The glass doors stood open on their balcony. Through these doors he could see the light on the mountains, which were barren and known as the Rockies, and toward morning the eastern slopes were pink with light. He got out of bed and stood for a while on the balcony. There was a good deal to see and to hear, as the city below him was rising, and in the blue morning light the woman on the bed seemed out of this world. Still wrapped in the

sheet, she looked prepared for burial. He dressed
in the bathroom, and when he came out her white
arm lay over her face, shutting out the light, so he
closed the doors to the balcony. What did he feel?
What he seemed to feel was concern for her.
Neither anger nor dislike, nor the emotions of a
man who had been a fool. No, he felt a certain
wonder, what you might call pity, for this man
once her husband, now dead, and for this woman,
his wife, who was still scared to death. He felt it,
that is, for both of them. They were out of this
world, certainly—but in what world were they
living? Greater than his anger, and his disappoint-
ment, was the wonder that he felt that there were
such people, and that they seemed to live, as he did,
in the same world. Their days in the open, but
their nights wrapped up in a sheet.

Practically speaking, a honeymoon is where you
adjust yourself to something, and Will Brady managed this adjustment in two weeks. He worked at
it. He gave it everything he had. He learned to
sleep, or to lie awake, indifferent to her. And when
he learned these things this woman, his wife, gave
up her sheet. There it was, back where it belonged,
between Will Brady and the woolly blanket, and
let it be said for him that he recognized it for what
it was. A compliment. Perhaps the highest he had
ever been paid.

The truth was that he was flattered, and it was her own suggestion, plainly made, that he learn to do the things her red-haired boy had done. Draw up her corset, and fasten the hooks at the side of her gowns. In the lobby this woman walked at his side, her hip brushing his own, and coming down from carriages she seemed loose in his arms. Another compliment? Well, he could take that too. He had taken something out of this world, learned to live with it. He had discovered, in this strange way, something about loving, about pity, and a good deal about hooks and eyes and corset strings.

He had this concern for her, and she seemed to be proud of him. Her handsome face was blank, with the pleasant vacant look again. They ate a good deal, in rooms overlooking the city, or in cool gardens with flowering plants, or they rode in buses to look with others at prominent views. It was not necessary, eating or looking, to say anything. Everything necessary had already been said.

If in three weeks' time two strangers can manage something like that, working together, who is to say what a year or two, or a summer, might bring? Who is to say what they might have made of something like that? But in three weeks' time he had to help her into her suit, with the hooks at both sides, and kneel on the floor and button her high traveling shoes. Then he held the ladder for her while she climbed into the upper berth. She was wearing a veil, the car was dark, and it might be said that the last he saw of the woman he knew was her high button shoes and the dusty hem of her petticoats. Whatever they had managed, between them, whatever they had made in the long three weeks, went up the ladder and never came down again. It remained, whatever it was, there in the berth. When she started down the next morning, calling for him to steady the ladder, the woman who spoke his name was a stranger again, his wife.

"Ethel," he said, taking her hand, "you're home again."

2

OVER the summer he liked to sleep in the spare room, with the window open, as he could see down the tracks to the semaphore. When the signals changed, this semaphore made a clicking sound. On quiet summer nights he would hear that sound and then roll on his side, rising on his elbow, to watch the coaches make a band of light on the plains. The rails would click, and when the train had passed, there would be little whirlwinds of dust and leaves, and a stranger might think that a storm was blowing up.

Beyond the semaphore was the cattle loader, the smell strong over the summer, and down the spur to the west, past the sawmill, the house of a man named Schultz. This man lived alone on a ten-acre farm. In his bedroom, along toward morning, a yellow lamp would be burning, and now and then the shadow of this man Schultz would move on the blind. A hard man, a bear for work, it was known that he had married a city girl, but that the caboose that had brought her to town also took her away. He kept the lamp burning, it was said, in case she came back.

An hour or so after the Flyer went by, the west-bound local came along from North Platte, and Will Brady had got into the habit of meeting it. Now and then important men stopped in Calloway. Once a month, for example, the local came along with T. P. Luckett, the man who had charge of the U.P. commissary in Omaha. A big man in every way, around two hundred sixty pounds, Mr. Luckett had his breakfast in the hotel, and while sitting in the lobby, smoking his cigar, he seemed to feel like talking with someone. At that time in the morning Will Brady was the only man there. In T. P. Luckett's opinion, that of a man who spoke frankly, Calloway was dead and didn't know it— a one-horse town with the horse ready for pasture, as he put it. Nebraska had spread itself too thin, he said, the western land was not particularly good, and what future there was, in anything but cattle, lay in the east. Within a day's ride from Omaha, that is. The whole state was tipped, T. P. Luckett said, low in the east, high in the west, and the best of everything had pretty well run off of it, like a roof. The good land was along the Missouri, near Omaha. The good men, as well, and in T. P. Luckett's opinion it was high time a young fellow like Will Brady gave it serious thought. Saw which way the wind was blowing, that is, and got off the dime. Calloway might always need a jerkwater hotel to meet the local, but a jerkwater man could take care of it. This fellow Luckett made it clear that a man like Will Brady, with his oversize head, was doing little more than wasting his time.

Will Brady had never thought of himself in such terms. Whether he was an up-and-coming man, and ought to be up-and-coming with the east, or whether what he was doing or not doing was wasting his time. He simply did it. That was the end of it. But it doesn't take a man long to acquire a taste for the better things. All he needs are these things. The taste comes naturally.

No, he had never given it a thought—but he did now. Running a hotel was little more than sitting in the lobby, between the potted palms, and facing the large railroad map of the state on the wall.

59

There on the map any man could see for himself.
There were ten towns in the east for every one in
the west. Did it matter? Well, it did when you
thought about it. When you're married, in a way,
and have settled down, and have stopped, in a way,
thinking about women, you find you have time now
and then to sit and think about something else. Your
future, for instance, and whether you're currently
wasting your time.

T. P. Luckett, for example, was a man who had
given up thinking about women in order to spend
all of his time thinking about eggs. He thought
about eggs because fresh eggs was one of the big
dining-car problems, and T. P. Luckett was the top
dining-car man. This problem kept a big man like
Luckett awake half the night. Wondering how he
could just put his hands on an honest-to-God fresh
egg. Eggs were always on this man's mind, and
perhaps it was natural that Will Brady, with nothing much on his mind, would get around to thinking about them. He made T. P. Luckett's problem
something of his own. Take those eggs he had for
breakfast, for instance; at one time he would have
eaten them, that was all, but now he examined the
shell, and marked the weight of each egg in his
hand. He broke them into a saucer to peer at the
yolk, examine it for small rings. He considered the
color of the eggs, and one morning he made the ob-

servation that the whites of some eggs, perhaps fresh ones, held their shape in the pan. Other eggs, perhaps older ones, had whites like milky water, the yolk poorly centered and slipping off to one side. T. P. Luckett thought this very interesting. *His* particular problem, T. P. Luckett said, looking at him in a friendly manner, was to determine something like that with the egg in the shell. Then he laughed, but he went on to say that any man who could study like that, his own eggs, that is, might well discover anything. He put his hand on Will Brady's shoulder, looking him straight in the eye, and forgot himself to the extent of offering him a good cigar.

A week or two later, toward morning, a time that Will Brady did most of this thinking, the solution to T. P. Luckett's problem occurred to him. The way to get grade-A fresh eggs was to lay them, on the spot. Get the chickens, the spot, and let the eggs be laid right there. Day-old eggs, which was about as fresh as an egg might be. All T. P. Luckett needed was a man to raise as many chickens as it took to lay the required number of eggs. That might be quite a few. But that's all he would need. This egg would be white, as the white egg, by and large, looked best in the carton, just as the rich yellow yolk looked best in the pan. And what chicken laid an egg like that? White Leghorns. It just so happened that a white chicken laid the whitest eggs.

T. P. Luckett listened to all of this without a word. A bald-headed man, he took off his straw and wiped the sweat off the top of his head, peered at the handkerchief, then stuffed it back in the pocket of his coat.

"All right, Will," he said, "you're the man."

"I'm what man?" he said.

"I've got five thousand dollars," T. P. Luckett said, "five thousand simoleons that says you're the man. That'll buy a lot of chickens, that'll even buy you some nice hens." Will Brady didn't have an answer to that. "Tell you what I'll do," T. P. Luckett said, "I'll throw in ten acres I've got near Murdock. Murdock is a lot better chicken country anyhow."

Will Brady had an answer to that. He said: "Mr. Luckett, I've got a wife and kids to think of. My wife has a home, several pieces of property right here."

"You think it over," T. P. Luckett said, and wiped his head again, put on his hat. "You think it over—right now you could sell all this stuff for what you got in it. Twenty years from now you won't be able to give it away."

"In a way," Will Brady said, "I like it here."

"Tell you what you do," T. P. Luckett said;

"you put the little woman in the buggy and some fine day you drive her over to Murdock, show her around. Leave it up to her if she wouldn't rather live in the east."

"I'll see what she says," Will Brady said.

"I'm not thinking of eggs. I'm thinking," T. P. Luckett said, "of a man of your caliber sitting around in the lobby of a jerkwater hotel."

"I'll think it over, Mr. Luckett," he said, and T. P. Luckett took off his hat, wiped his head with the sleeve of his shirt, put his hat on, and went out.

As a man could marry only one woman, Will Brady had once brooded over such matters as the several thousand women he would have to do without. As no one woman had everything, in the widest sense of the term, neither did any egg have everything. But he came to the conclusion, after months of consideration, that the Leghorn egg had the most for the "carriage trade." This was how T. P. Luckett referred to those people who were something. What we've got to keep in mind, he always said, is how the carriage trade will like it. A very neat way of putting things, once you thought about it. Will Brady had seen a good many of such people through the wide windows of the diners, and on occasion he had spoken to some of them. Offering a match, or the time of day, as the case might be. It was very easy to tell such men from those who dipped their napkins in their water glasses, then used the napkin to clean their celluloid collars, their false cuffs. With a little experience a man could tell the real carriage trade from that sort of people, as easily as the real carriage trade could tell a good egg. Nine out of ten times it would be a Leghorn.

Well, that was the egg, but what about the chicken laying it? Did it take two, maybe three of them, to lay one egg? Did they quit after a while, die over the winter, or get the croup? To determine these and like matters, he bought three dozen Leghorn hens, kept them in sheds behind the barn, and bought a ledger to keep their record in. This ledger he kept in the basement, and every evening he entered the number of eggs, the amount of grain eaten, and the proportion of large eggs to the case. He compared this with the figures at the local creamery. Every morning he cracked two eggs, peered at the yolks, then fried them, slowly, in butter, or he boiled them and served them in an official dining-car cup. He had never been of much use with his hands, he hurt himself with hammers, cut himself with knives, but it seemed that he could handle an egg with the best of them. He could take five in each hand, right out of the case, and hold them gently, not a shell cracking, or he could take two eggs, crack them, and fry them with one hand. There were people who would like to have seen that, his wife perhaps, and certainly T. P. Luckett, but he did it alone, just as a matter of course, every morning. He studied eggs, just as a matter of course, every night. As all of his own eggs were fresh and didn't need to be candled, he had a case of cold-storage eggs sent out from Omaha. He mixed them up with his own eggs, then sorted them out. It took him several weeks, but he learned—without anyone around to tell him—how a fresh egg *looked*, and about how old a storage egg was.

In April he took a Sunday off to drive his wife over to Murdock, a town of several thousand people and some big shady trees. Just east of town was a two-way drive with a strip of grass right down the middle, lamps on concrete posts, and a sign welcoming visitors to town. There was nothing to compare with it in Calloway. T. P. Luckett's ten acres were just a half mile north of town. A nice flat piece of ground, it lay between the new road and the curve of the railroad, and there was plenty room for several thousand laying hens, maybe more. Along the north side of the land was a fine windbreak of young cottonwood trees.

They had their dinner in town, at a Japanese restaurant where there were paintings on the walls, and violin music played throughout the meal. They sat in a booth, with a dim light on the table, and though his wife had once been in St. Louis, and seen many fine things, it was clear she had seen nothing like this. At the front of the restaurant was a glass case, with a slot at one side for a coin, and on dropping a coin the violin in the case would begin to play. One hand held the bow, the other plucked the strings. As she was very fond of music he walked forward twice and played it for her.

At the end of this meal he told her what he had in mind. He described, pretty much in detail, what T. P. Luckett had told him, and how Calloway, inside of twenty years, would be a dead town. A man of his caliber, he said, quoting T. P. Luckett, had no business wasting his life in a jerkwater hotel. He had meant to say small, not jerkwater, but when he got there the word came out, and he saw that it made quite an impression on her. She had never seen the hotel, or the town, in quite that light before. Perhaps she hadn't thought of him, her husband, as a man of caliber. It made a lasting impression on her, and while they sat there a Mr. Tyler, the man who owned the restaurant, presented her, absolutely free, with a souvenir. This was a booklet describing the town of Murdock. There were thirty-two pages, every page with a picture, and at the back of the booklet was a table showing how all the real-estate values were shooting up. On the cover was the greeting:

WELCOME TO
MURDOCK
THE
BIGGEST
LITTLE TOWN IN THE WORLD

and while she glanced through it he walked back
to play the magic violin again.

3

IN THE town of Murdock Will Brady bought a
house with a room at the front, which he used to
sleep in, and a room at the back where he ate his
meals. Once a week, however, he would take his
family to the Japanese restaurant, sit them in a
booth, and give the boys coins to play for their
mother the magic violin. His wife, Ethel, liked to
sit where she could see the wax hand move the real
bow. Will Brady took the seat facing the window
where the yokels that stood along the curb would
walk back and press their noses to the glass and
peer in at them. He had never really thought much
about these people, the kids off the farms and the
old men still on them, until he sat there in the booth
and saw their corn-fed faces grinning at him. Then

he knew that they were yokels, corn-fed hicks from the ground up.

That's what they were, but with the war coming on, things were looking up. Sometimes a farmer with six or seven kids would bring them into town, herd them into the restaurant, but leave his wife in the buggy until she had finished nursing the little one. Will Brady could see that buggy through the window, and it would be new, the spokes would be red, and there might be a new creaking set of harness on the old horse. The horse would toss his head to get the feed at the bottom of his new feed bag. And the woman in the buggy might have a new hat, a Sears Roebuck print dress, or the high button shoes that he could see when she lifted her skirts from the buggy wheel.

And at the edge of town, where there had once been weeds, or maybe nothing at all to speak of, there was now a field of grain or a new crop of beans. Every acre that would grow weeds had been plowed up. And it was no passing thing, people had to eat—hadn't Will Brady himself just read somewhere that the rich Missouri Valley was going to be the bread basket of the world? The world had to eat something, so it might as well be eggs. Fresh, day-old eggs if possible. Somewhere else he had read, or heard a man say, that there were more than four hundred million Chinamen who had never had a really square meal in their lives. Well, an up-and-coming man like Will Brady would give it to them. All that had to be done was to stop them eating rice, start them eating eggs.

In the old country this Kaiser fellow had done a lot of damage and killed a lot of people, but in the new country he seemed to be doing a lot of good. Will Brady could see it on the faces of the men who came into town. This war boom was about the finest thing that had happened to them. Some of the women might feel a little different, but it was hard to complain about a new buggy, a roof for the barn, and a machine that would separate the milk from the cream. And now and then a tired farm woman liked to eat out. She liked to see her new baby in the red high chairs that came along with the meal, like the cups and plates, and sit there at the table with her own two hands free to eat. Nothing in her lap but the folded napkin and the bones for the dog. Just a year or two before, this same woman came to town in the wagon, with the tailboard down, but now she rode in a tassel-fringed buggy with a spring seat. And having tasted the finer things in life, like Will Brady, she would go on wanting them.

4

THE HOUSE Will Brady bought had five other rooms besides those he ate and slept in, but he didn't have much to do with them. The house was usually dark in the morning when he left it, and again in the evening when he got home, and rather than fool around with the lamp, he undressed in the dark. The wick of the lamp was charred and left an oily smell in the air.

Was he all right? Once a week his wife, Ethel, asked him that. She spoke to him through the bedroom door, the lamp shadow at her feet. Yes, he was all right—just a little preoccupied. That was it, he was just a little preoccupied.

There was a window at the foot of his bed, but he kept the blind drawn because the street light, swinging over the corner, sometimes kept him awake. As the chairs were hard to see in the dark, he kept one of them in the corner, and the other at the side of the bed for his watch and coat. Sometimes he put his pants there too if he happened to think of it. Otherwise he dropped them on the floor, or folded them over the rail at the foot of the bed, with his collar and tie looped around the brass post. He slept in his socks, but that was not something new—he had always done that. It helped keep his feet warm and also saved quite a bit of time.

The room was always dark, but if he lay awake he could make out the calendar over the stovepipe hole, the white face of the clock, and the knobs on the dresser from Calloway. But the grain of the bird's-eye maple was lost on him. On the dresser was a bottle of cherry cough syrup, which he took when he had an upset stomach, a comb and a brush, and a very large Leghorn egg. This egg had three yolks, but he couldn't decide what to do with it. As it was ten days old, he would soon have to make up his mind. At the foot of the bed, in the cream-colored wall, he could see the door that he used twice a day, and on hot summer nights he left it open to start a cool draft. The rest of the time he kept it closed, with the key in the lock.

It might be going too far to say that Will Brady lived in this house, as he spent his time elsewhere and usually had other things on his mind. But he came back there every night, went away from there every morning, and something like that, if you keep at it, gets to mean something. There were always, for instance, clean shirts in the dresser drawer. There were always socks with the holes mended, and if they had just been washed this woman, his wife, first ran her hand into each one of them.

There were always collar studs in the cracked saucer beside the clock. When he was sick, or coughed in the night, or was found there in bed the following morning, the woman of the house came to the door of his room and knocked. She would give him hot lemonade and sound advice. The blinds would be raised to let in the sunshine, his coat and pants would be hung on the door, and she would ask him—after looking for them—for his socks. She always found it hard to believe that they were still on his feet.

The woman of the house lived at the back, in a large sunny room full of plants and flowers, but the children of the house seemed to live with the neighbors, or under the front porch. They went there to eat candy, drink strawberry pop, and divide up the money they took from his pockets on Sundays, holidays, and any other time he had to change his pants. In the evening Will Brady sometimes stopped to peer under the porch, and wonder about it, as nothing ever seemed to be there but the soft hot dust. The lawnmower and the wooden-runner sled were pushed far to the back.

Other evenings Will Brady might stop in the alley and look at the yard, the three white birch trees, and the house that had now been paid for, every cent of it. It looked quite a bit like the neighboring houses in most respects. It had a porch at the front, lightning rods, a peaked roof, panes of colored glass; and in the rooms where the lights were on, the blinds were always drawn. Homelike? Well, that was said to be the word for it. And after a certain hour all of the lights in the house would be out. The people in the house would do what they could to go to sleep. By some common agreement, since there was no law saying that they had to, they would turn out the lights, go to bed, and try to sleep. Or they would lie there making out the shape of things on the wall. Why did they do it? Well, it was simply how things were done. It was one of those habits that turned out to be pretty hard to break.

Will Brady often wondered—when he didn't sleep—what the man in the neighboring house was doing, if he slept well himself, or if he came home and undressed in the dark. This man was a prominent citizen. He had just installed a new marble fountain in his store. Revolving stools, on white enamel posts, sat in front of it. During the evening his daughter, a large pasty girl, would wipe off the counter and the marble-topped tables, and Mr. Kirby himself would walk around and push the wire-legged chairs back into place. A little stout, in his forties somewhere, Clyde Kirby always spoke to you by name, asked about the missus, and sent you one of his New Year calendars. Hard to say, offhand, whether he undressed in the dark or not. He had raised five sons and was old enough to have learned a thing or two.

Will Brady sometimes stood in the alley adjoining Clyde Kirby's house. The blinds were usually drawn, as they were in his own, but one evening the windows were up and he saw Clyde Kirby, with his sleeves rolled up, standing in the pantry door. He was crumbling hunks of cornbread into a tall drinking glass. He filled this glass to the top with cornbread, then he took a can of milk, punched two holes, and poured the heavy cream over the cornbread, filling the glass. With the handle of his spoon, like a soda boy, he slushed it up and down. He seemed to be in a hurry, for some reason, but before he could lift the spoon to his mouth he heard a noise in the house, a door at the front had opened and closed. And like a kid who had got into the jam pot, this Clyde Kirby, a leading citizen, took the glass of cornbread he was holding and hid it behind his back. He just stood there, as if he was thinking, while the woman of the house came out of the hallway and carefully drew the blinds clear around the living-room. One by one she drew down all of the blinds on that side of the house. Then she entered the kitchen, walking past Mr. Kirby like a propped-up ironing board, and drew the blinds around the kitchen, hooked the screen, then went back the way she had come. All of this without making a gesture, without saying a word. And Clyde Kirby stood there, the glass at his back, until he heard the door at the front snap closed, then he crossed the dark kitchen and stood at the sink. He poured more canned milk over the cornbread, slushed it up and down with the spoon, then stood there gulping it down as though he was starved to death.

If it was the man's business to eat in the kitchen, it seemed to be the woman's business to keep the blinds drawn, and to make out of what went on in the house a home. For good or bad, a man seemed to need a woman around the house. And if Will Brady was a father, then this woman he had married was a mother of sorts.

Concerning his fatherhood, Will Brady sometimes walked from the front of the house to the back, tapped on the door, and with a serious face then put in his head. This woman he had married would be sitting there, mending clothes. Will Brady would say what he had to say—something about the poisons in penny candy—and she would agree with him, this woman, that the poisons were there. But the pimples, if that's what he meant, didn't mean anything. All boys had them. And that was what he wanted to hear. The poisons in penny candy were a man's business, and when he spoke she respected him for it; but the pimples on the chin were a woman's business, and he respected her. And it was up to her to make, out of all of this business, something called a home.

Well, that was the woman's business, but what about his own? If you want to get the feel of the egg business you take an egg in your hand—that is, you take thousands of them—and from each egg you slowly chip off the hen spots with your thumb. It isn't really necessary to candle the egg or peer around inside. The necessary thing is to get the feel of an egg in your hand.

That's how it is with eggs, but chickens are something else. A few old hens in the yard are one thing, but when you take a thousand pullets, say several thousand Leghorn pullets, what you have on your hands is something else. To get the feel of something like that troubled a lot of men. No man would rein in his horse to look at one chicken, but there were sometimes four or five buggies, or a wagonful of kids, drawn off the road just east of the Brady chicken farm. On Sunday afternoons even the women would be there. Five thousand Leghorn pullets was something no man had been able to describe. There was nothing to do but put

the family in the buggy, let them see it for themselves.

They were usually farm people for the most
part, people who ought to be sick to death of
chickens, but they would get in their buggies and
ride for half a day just to look at them. Some of
these families brought their lunches and made a
picnic out of it. Monday morning the ditch grass
would be short where the grazing horses had
clipped it, and the road would be scarred where
the buggy weights had dragged in the dust. As
these people didn't know Will Brady from Adam,
he was free to drive his own team right in among
them, let his mares graze, and look on with the rest
of them. Five thousand Leghorns, five acres of
white feathers, if a man could speak in terms like
that. And why not? Somehow he had to describe
this thing. Or perhaps a sea of feathers, a lake of
whitecaps, when the wind caught them from the
back, fanning out their tails and blowing loose
feathers along with the dust. Will Brady used the
word, though of course he had never seen the sea.
Nor had he ever seen a larger body of water than
Carter Lake. It was simply that the word came to
mind, and Will Brady often spoke of his sea of
chickens the way other men would refer to a field
of corn. If and when he saw the sea, very likely he

would think it looked like that. He would gaze out on the water and see five thousand pullets that would soon be hens.

There were also some sheds, which seemed to float like so many small boats in the sea of feathers, and there was a bare clearing where he planned to erect a fine city house. But from the buggies men saw just the chickens, the high unpainted cable fence, and the green bank of the railroad like a dam to hold it all in. Different men, of course, saw different things, but perhaps the best way to describe it was a remark that T. P. Luckett let drop one day.

"How's your empire, Brady?" he said, and most people let it go at that.

5

Once a month he went to Omaha on business, what you might call a business investment, as he found he worked better if he got away from Murdock now and then. The life in the city seemed to stimulate him. He always took a room at the Wellington Hotel, where there were fine potted palms in the lobby, a large map on the wall, and where altogether he felt more or less at home. He would sit between the palms, facing the street, or he would swing the chair around and face the lobby, the elevator cage, and the cigar-counter girl. She would usually be rattling the dice in the leather cup, or kidding with the old men. Summer evenings he might walk out on the new bridge and look at the bluffs across the river, or at the swirling brown water, more like mud than water, that he saw below. T. P. Luckett had said that part of the state was washing away. Standing there on the bridge Will Brady could see the truth of that. On his walk back to the hotel he would pick up a jar of hard candy for the boys, and make arrangements for the flowers, the roses, he would take to his wife.

"Would the gentleman like to include a card?" the flower girl always said.

"No," he would say, "no, thank you—it's just for my wife."

If the weather was bad he would sit in the lobby facing the girl behind the cigar counter and observing the way she had learned to handle the men. These men were all older, by and large, being traveling men with a sharp sense of humor, but she had learned to talk right back to them without batting an eye. Most of the men played dice with her for cigars. The dice were held in a leather cup, where they made a hollow rattle like peas in a gourd, and after the rattle she would roll them out on a small green pad. The older men liked to do it, it seemed, whether they won or not. The girl would slide back the glass top to the case and the man would reach in, helping himself to a La Paloma or whatever brand he liked. At the side of the counter was a small lamp, in a hood to keep the flame from blowing, and on a chain was a knife with a blade for snipping off the tip of your cigar. They would then purse their lips like a fat hen's bottom as they moistened the tip. It seemed to give these men a great deal of satisfaction just to rattle the dice, win or lose, and to help themselves to a cigar from the glass case. The hollow sound of the dice could be heard in the lobby, and in his room on the second floor, if the transom was down, Will Brady could hear the game being played. The men usually laughed, a booming manly laugh, if the girl won.

Although he neither smoked nor gambled Will Brady seemed to like the sound of the dice, and something or other about the game seemed to interest him. Perhaps he had a yen to take the leather cup in his hand, shake it himself. To see if he could roll a seven, an eleven, or whatever it was. When the girl won, as she usually did, she would often wink at somebody in the lobby—at Will Brady if he happened to be sitting there. Although he didn't gamble, he would wink back at her. It was something she did with all the old men: it didn't mean anything. The day she spoke to him, for example, she was just playing the game with herself, she didn't trouble to wink, she just spoke to him right out of the blue.

"Come and have a game on me," she said.

"I don't play," he replied, but in a friendly manner.

"Come and play for a good cigar," she said, and rattled the dice. "Three," she said, "you can surely beat a three."

"Maybe," he said, "but I don't smoke."

"You don't what?" she said.

"I don't smoke," he replied.

The girl put down the leather cup she was holding and looked at him. "You're just kidding," she said, "what's your brand? I'll bet it's La Paloma for a man like you."

"Thank you very much," he said, "but I don't smoke." She looked at him for a while, and he looked back at her. She winked at him, but of course it didn't mean anything.

"You don't play either?" she said.

"No," he said, "I don't play."

She rattled the dice in the cup, then said: "You don't play, you don't smoke—what do you do?"

"I work," Will Brady replied, as if that explained everything, and maybe it did. He had never put it just that way before. "I work," he repeated, and smiled at the girl, but this time she didn't wink.

"If you don't smoke, why don't you smoke?" she said.

"I suppose I never started," he said; "if you don't start, maybe you don't want to."

"You really think so?"

"Well, I don't smoke," he said.

"I thought maybe you didn't smoke for your wife," she said. As he didn't get the point of that right away, Will Brady turned and looked at the lobby. When he got it, he said:

"I don't think my wife cares very much."

"I would," she said, "I would if I had any choice." Before he could think of an answer to that another man, about his own age, stepped up to the counter and pushed back the glass top to the case. He helped himself to a cigar, moistened the tip, then went off chewing on it. "You see what I mean?" the girl said, and made a face. When Will Brady didn't answer, she said: "Just imagine kissing something like that."

Turning to face the lobby Will Brady replied: "Well, I hear that some of them do."

"They don't if they have any choice," said the girl, and rattled the dice. He didn't have an answer to that, so she said: "—but I guess they don't have much choice. What choice do you have when some men never take a day off?"

"What would a man want to take a day off for?" he said.

"It's a good thing I don't take you men seriously," she replied.

As he wanted to be taken seriously, he said: "I've never had a day off in my life."

"You men!" she said, and made a clucking sound with her tongue.

"A day off—" he said, "what for?"

"I like men who wear red ties," she said.

He looked down at his new red tie, then he replied: "Not every man can take a day off, but there's some men who can if they want to. Men of a certain caliber are more or less free to do as they like."

"If they don't smoke," she said, "I suppose they've got to do something." She winked at him, and this time he winked back. "That's why I wish I was a man," she said; "a man can do as he likes, but a woman only has one day a week."

"What day is that?" he said, and looked her right in the eye.

"Friday," she said, looking right back at him, "I'm off every Friday at five o'clock." She rolled the dice out on the pad, and when it turned up a four and a three she said: "That means it's lucky for me. What kind of car does a man like you drive?"

Several years before, listening to T. P. Luckett, something of this sort had come over Will Brady, and he had become, overnight almost, a man of caliber. Now he became the owner of a car. An Overland roadster—one of the kind that a man like himself might drive.

He bought this car in Columbus, where he had to change trains, and the new Willys-Overland dealer had a fine big showroom facing the station and the tracks. In the window was the Overland roadster with the sporty wire wheels. They were red, and about the same color as his tie.

As he stood there listening to the powerful motor he let the owner of the shop persuade him that he might as well get into the car and drive it home. On west of Columbus it was wide-open country, there was nothing but horses to worry about, and the only way to learn to drive a car was to get in and drive. Once he got in, and got the car moving, he would find that the Overland drove itself, leaving nothing for the driver to do but sit there and shift the gears. At the railroad crossings he would get a lot of practice in.

He got in a lot of practice, all right, but some of

it was lost owing to the fact that he drove along, thirty miles or so, in second gear. The road was so bad that he didn't seem to notice it. Ten miles an hour was pretty good time over most of it. It was just getting dark when he came into Murdock, at the edge of the Chautauqua grounds, where he saw that several boys had built a bonfire near the tracks. One of them, a very spry little fellow, was hopping around. Now, boys often behave like that and he might not have thought anything of it if he hadn't noticed, in the light from the fire, that he had on no pants. He was hopping up and down, hollering and yelling, without his pants. When Will Brady saw who this spry boy was, and what it was they all seemed to be doing, his hand went forward, in spite of himself, and honked the horn. They jumped up like rabbits, every one of them, and ran for the trees. But not a single boy, and there were maybe ten of them, had on his pants. They ran off like madmen, hooting like Indians, through the scrubby willows along the tracks, and bringing up the rear, his bottom bright in the car lights, was Will Brady's son. Farther down the tracks they picked up their pants and ran along waving them, like banners, but there was not time, of course, to stop and put them on. Will Brady just sat there till he heard the motor running, and the hooting had passed.

Perhaps that was why he went to Omaha again the following week. He had it in mind to walk down lower Douglas, where he knew there were doctors "for men," and speak to one of these doctors about the strange behavior of the boys. He had often seen the signs that were painted on the windows on the second floor. So he walked along this street, he read the signs, but he couldn't seem to make up his mind how to describe what had happened, or whether Willy Brady, aged nine, was a man or not. These doctors for men might think that Will Brady was kidding them. He went back and took a seat in the lobby of the Wellington Hotel. It happened to be Saturday, not Friday, but the girl behind the counter had been thinking it over, and she wondered if Sunday wouldn't be a better time for him. Now that he had a car, and in case he really wanted to take the day off.

If there were people in Murdock who had picked up the notion that Will Brady liked other chickens as well as Leghorns, talk like that somehow never got around to him. It couldn't, as he seldom talked to anyone. Not that Will Brady wasn't friendly— everybody remarked how friendly he was—but he didn't have the time, or whatever it took, to make friends. Will Brady was what they called a go-getter, a man who not only was up and coming, but in a lot of things, the important things, had already arrived. Just north of town, for example, he had a chicken farm with five thousand Leghorns, and on a cold windy day some of the feathers even blew into town. And work had begun on his modern thirteen-room house. As illustrated in *Radnor's Ideal Homes,* Will Brady's house would have a three-story tower, and was listed under "Mansions," the finest section of the book. Not listed, but to be part of the house, were the diamond-shaped panes of colored glass, imported from Chicago like the marble in Clyde Kirby's new drugstore. As there were thirty-six windows in this house, including those in the basement and the tower, there would be nothing like it in either Murdock or Calloway. If there was light, it came through a panel of colored glass. If there was no light, as sometimes couldn't be helped, a lantern would be burning in the top of the tower, shining through a green porthole like the semaphore far down the tracks. A man out on the plains could get his bearings just by looking at it.

This fellow Brady was a comer, as everybody said, but not many people would have recognized him, or the girl along with him, on certain warm summer nights. Out in the Krug Amusement Park he would sit on a bench, holding her cone of spun sugar candy, while she rode the roller coaster and other up-and-down rides that made him sick. Early in the evening she would first go swimming, leaving him on the beach with her comb and her lipstick, or in the wicker chairs for parents on the balcony behind the diving board. Before diving she would turn and wave to him. Chased by boys, she liked to swim under water, and in his anxiety Will Brady would rise out of the chair and somebody would ask him to please sit down. There were other people who had children to account for, this man would say.

Elderly folks, both men and women, often drew up their chairs to speak to Will Brady, ask about his girl, and tell him what a fine-looking child she was. When he agreed, they would point out youngsters of their own. Most of them were plump, good-looking girls, squealing like pigs when the boys edged near them, and Will Brady could see that nearly all parents had the same concern. To be there to wave when the children dived, to tell them when they turned the soft blue color, and to shoo off the boys, like flies, when they sprawled out on the sand. Later would come the Ferris wheel, the Spook House, the balls thrown at something, and if it was hit he would carry the Kewpie doll. He would spend five dollars to win a fifty-cent Ouija board. In the ballroom, with these things in his lap, he would sit on a folding chair in the corner watching her dance with some young buck who had asked her to. A youngster who thought *he* was her father, naturally. And they would bring him a hot dog, a bottle of red pop, and stand there before him, trying to be friendly, looking over their shoulders at the young people who danced.

"Now, why don't you kids go and dance," he would say, and while they did he would eat the hot dog and look at the Ouija board, as the boy would be hugging her. But not too much, as he *was* her father, and after a while the boy would bring her back, shake Will Brady's hand, and try to leave a good impression with him.

"I'm very glad to have met you, sir," these boys would say.

But after the swimming, the riding, and the dancing, she would play with him. She would take him for several long rides on the Swanee River, that is. Will Brady found it spooky and unpleasant, the rocking of the boat troubled him, but on the whole he got along without getting sick. And in the dark part of the river, in the mossy wood, where the water splashed over the mill wheel, she would take his hands in her own and put them around her waist. There she would hold them, tight, until they reached the pier where the ride had ended, and everybody on the pier could see how it was with the pair in the boat. That this man with the straw hat was a good deal more than a father to her. He was her lover. A man to be pitied and envied, that is.

To make it perfectly clear who Will Brady was, she needed help with her clothes in lobbies and restaurants, and out on the street dust was always blowing into her eyes. She would have to press against him while he saw what the trouble was. In the aisles of big stores she liked to swoon, as the high-class ladies swooned in the movies, and to have him come with her while she shopped for stockings and underclothes. Nobody had taught her how to wear clothes so that she looked covered when she had them on, but she had learned from her mother how to go without them and look all right. Like swimming under water, it astonished and troubled him. Her mother was an actress on the vaudeville circuit, and her father was one of five men, in a ten-minute act, who entered the room and hid under the bed. Will Brady had once seen her mother, on a poster, on lower Douglas Street. Her daughter looked a good deal like her in most respects.

There was little resemblance, certainly, between this girl and sad-eyed Opal Mason, but at night he had the feeling Opal Mason would approve of her. Like Opal Mason, the girl liked to talk. Will Brady often had the feeling that he was there in bed for reasons he hadn't really looked into and were not at all the reasons that an outsider might think. He never said much himself, as he was too sleepy and felt he was there for fairly obvious reasons, but toward morning, without her saying anything, he would wake up. Why was that? It seemed to be because she wanted him to. He couldn't really do much for her, somehow, but one thing he could do was wake up in the morning, roll on his back, and lie there listening to her. Sometimes he wondered if this might be another form of loving, one that women needed, just as men seemed to need the more obvious kind. But he didn't really know, and the talking never cleared it up. As a matter of fact, the more she talked, the less he understood.

Sometimes this girl would begin with the morning and describe everything that had happened; she would describe, that is, every man who had troubled to follow her. She remembered and described these men so well that Will Brady, who saw very little, would recognize these men as the familiar fops he passed in the street. Every one of them useless, whore-chasing men, with a gold-toothed smile, light-tan button shoes, and a pin in his tie he could buy for fifteen cents. And they were all, she insisted, very fine gentlemen. When he scoffed at this she wanted to know what he would know about men like that, not knowing anybody, let alone classy people like that. Then she would go on—she always went on—to tell him that a lady knew a gentleman by the oil in his hair and the fancy silk socks that he wore. And the way that he would stand, in the better-class lobbies, shooting his cuffs.

Well, there were things that he might have said, but he would have to lie there, his mouth tight shut, as right there on the floor, at the side of the bed, were his own dirty socks. Or worse yet, they might still be on his feet, right there in the bed. What could he say—a man like that—about fine gentlemen? Nor could he even ask her where she had picked up such notions. He knew, for one thing—he knew she had smelled this hair at close quarters, snapped the cuff links herself, and praised the gentlemen's taste in socks. He knew, and it was the last thing in the world he cared to hear about.

If she liked these dandies, he had said, and he liked the word *dandy*, what in the world did she see in a man like him?

"Your hair," she had replied. Just like that. That had made him so mad he said what he had on his mind.

"And how are these dandies to sleep with?" he said.

"Oh," she said, "like anybody." But as he lay back she added: "But what's that to do with what I like?"

* * *

In the Clearing

As he drove into Omaha every Friday and home again on Sunday evening, he may have picked up the notion that it might go on indefinitely. Now and then he did wonder about the girl, and the five days a week he wasn't there to watch her, but he neither wondered nor worried about his wife. She lived in the sunny room at the back of the house, and when she heard him come in, on Sunday evening, she would call out: "Is that you, Will?" and he would answer: "Yes, Ethel," and hook the screen, turn out the light. Then he would walk through the dark house to his room at the front.

The night she didn't call out, his first thought was that she might be asleep. He didn't worry about it until he got into bed, when the quiet of the house, something or other about it, and the creaking street light seemed to keep him awake. The night, he thought, seemed quieter than usual. That might have been because of the noise of the city, where a street car passed right below the window, but it kept him awake like the lull that follows a wind. He sat up in bed at one point and looked out. He could see the gnats and hear the big fat June bugs strike the street light. Turning from the window he noticed the door that led from his room into the boy's, and on the chair in front of the door were his pants. On holidays, when he might sleep late, the boy would open the door and take some of the small change from his pants. Was that stealing? Neither of them had mentioned it.

It occurred to Will Brady that it had been some time since the boy had come in to swipe a little money, or since his father had opened the door to question the boy. Not since the week the boy had taken to drinking vinegar. He would take the big vinegar jug to his room, hiding it beneath the bed or inside of his pillow, and when the lights were out he would pull out the cork and take a swig. Later he would be sick and vomit over his Teddy bears. It had been a very strange thing to do—like the hooting and howling with his pants off—but Dr. Finley had said some boys would surprise you. And they certainly would.

At that time Will Brady had suggested that the door between their rooms might be left open, but the boy said his father's snoring kept him awake. Perhaps it did. So the door was closed again. But there was no more vinegar trouble and for a while everything seemed all right, until Will Brady came home one night and found the entire house lit up. The boy was propped up in bed with his bears, but his hair was shaved off. He had dipped his head, with all of his lovely curls, in a barrel of hot tar. Several men had been repairing the roof of the church, and while they were up there working on

it, the boy had sneaked over and dipped his head in
their barrel of tar. God knows how he had ever
thought of something like that. A crazy thing to
do, but he had done it, and the long silken curls
that hung below his shoulders were thrown away
with the stiff chunks of tar. The top of his small,
narrow head had to be shaved. He looked like a
bird that had just been hatched, and it upset Ethel,
who was not his real mother, a good deal more than
it did the boy. She took to bed for several days herself. It might be that Ethel, who already had a boy,
had wanted a small pretty girl for a change, as she
let his hair grow and liked to dress him in rompers
and Fauntleroys. But the tar had put an end to that.

With his small head shaved Willy Brady was
neither a boy nor a girl. In the evening his father
would sometimes open the door and look into the
room, where the lamp sat on the table, and the boy
would be sitting there in bed with his three brown
bears. One of them, the papa bear, almost as big as
he was. And always reading, as *they* had just
learned to read. As Will Brady didn't want to dis-
turb them—the three bears had staring glass eyes—
he would close the door without saying anything.
Standing there in the dark, he would hear the boy
whisper to one of them.

Although he had never done it before, he got out
of bed, lit his lamp, and opened the door to the

boy's room. He first thought the figure propped up in bed was the boy, with his eyes wide open, but it turned out to be the papa bear. The boy was not there in the bed at all. But pinned to the bear's woolly chest was a piece of note paper, torn from a pad, that seemed to be blank until he came forward with the lamp. It was not signed, nor did it say to whom it was addressed, but Will Brady recognized the writing well enough. His wife, Ethel, wrote a fine Spencerian hand.

Willy is with Mrs. Riddlemosher

it said, and that was all. That was all he ever heard from Ethel Czerny Bassett, his wife.

6

WITH a small pail of sand containing horsetail hairs that would turn to garter snakes when it rained on them, Will Brady and his son moved from the town of Murdock to the city of Omaha. They took a room on the mezzanine floor of the Wellington Hotel. The pail of sand was kept at the front of the lobby, behind the tub with the potted palm, so that Willy Brady, in case it rained, could

run outside with it. Sometimes he did, other times
he just let it rain.

In the morning the boy would be there in the
lobby, sitting near one of the brass spittoons, where
he was told he could whittle or spit the black
licorice juice. Most of the time he just sat there,
with his legs straight out. The women who worked
in the hotel restaurant would stop and speak to him.

After lunch, with his friend Mr. Wherry, he
would play four or five games of checkers, or a
game of parcheesi with the cigar-counter girl. It
might be that Mr. Wherry, who was fond of children, thought the girl behind the counter was the
boy's sister, as he seemed to think they were both
Will Brady's kids. He bought them bags of candy
and took them down the street to the matinee. He
was a fine old man, but a little hard of hearing; and
something like that, a problem like that, was better
left alone, as it might prove hard to explain.

If the boy wasn't there in the lobby he might be
on the mezzanine, in the phone booth, having long
conversations with the telephone girl. He would
leave word with her to have his father call him
when he came in.

"This is Willy Brady Jr.," the voice would say,
with the confident tone of a Singer's midget, and
somehow his father, Will Brady, was never pre-

pared for it. He would stand there, and the boy would say: "Who is this speaking?"

"This is your father, son," Will Brady would say, in the sober voice of a father, but he never had the feeling that the boy was impressed. He didn't believe it any more than Willy Brady did himself.

Once a week, as a father should, he would borrow the boy from Mr. Wherry and take him to the places a boy would like to go. This was usually to see a man named Eddie Polo, whom they left in some pit, every week, as good as dead, only to come back the next week and find him big as life. The boy was also crazy about Charlie Chaplin, but he had seen everything a good many times, and made a nuisance of himself as he always got the hiccups when he laughed. He would have to be led back to the lobby, many times, for a drink. As Will Brady didn't care for Eddie Polo himself, any more than he did for the roller coaster, he would pass the time eating the popcorn or peanuts he bought for the boy. As he couldn't get his hand in the small-size bag, he had to buy the large-size ones, and near the middle of the movie he usually wanted a drink himself. They would both have a phosphate, usually cherry, at the drugstore when they got out.

Summer evenings, if it was still light after they had got out of the movie, he might walk the boy down Farnam Street to the Market Place. Will

Brady's place of business faced the west, and if it wasn't too late in the evening some light from the sky might be on the new sign he had at the front. This sign cost him three hundred dollars, and featured two roosters, drawn by hand, crowing over a large Leghorn egg. Through a misunderstanding both of the birds were Plymouth Rocks, as well as roosters—a point that troubled Will Brady, but the boy never noticed it. He didn't seem to care what color the eggs, or the chickens, were. On the wide glass window, lettered in gold, were the words:

WILL BRADY
EGGS

but the boy never seemed to realize that name was his own. That one day it would read WILL BRADY & SON. Any number of times, as they came around the corner, Will Brady meant to bring it up, but when they got there and stood facing the building, nothing was said. There seemed to be no connection. Perhaps that was it. There they were, Father & Son, looking through the window of their future—but it seemed to be Will Brady's, not the boy's. He never walked up and pressed his nose to the window, as most boys would do, and he didn't seem to care what went on behind the glass. If Will Brady said: "Now just a minute, son," and felt around in his pocket for the keys, the boy would stand out on the curbing while he went in. Sometimes he made quite a racket to attract attention, or stood in the candling-room, holding some eggs, but the boy never came back to see what was delaying him.

No, the only person that seemed to care, or wonder what it was he was doing, was the old man who sometimes slept in the back of the shop. A drifter, a wreck of a man with a dark bearded face, and one hand missing, he would sometimes get up from where he was lying and come peer at him. He would open the flap to the candling-room and put in his head. There he would be, a strange smile on his face, and perhaps a nail in one corner of his mouth, looking in on Will Brady as if he had called for him. Wagging his head, this old man would say: "Mr. Brady, how's that boy of yours?"

And it had turned out the old man had a boy of his own. Older, of course. Gone off somewhere, that is. A boy who had a mother who had also gone off somewhere. This old man probably didn't understand some of the words Will Brady fell to using, but he had been a father, and seemed to know the way of boys. He would wag his head as if it was all familiar to him. His own name he never mentioned, but a boy named Gregor, and a girl named Pearl, were very much like their mother, a woman named Belle. At the thought of her he would reach for the nail keg, put more nails in his mouth.

The old man kept the stub of his arm in his pocket, but speaking of war, which he knew at first hand, he would draw it out, like a sword, and point with it. The missing hand seemed to be something, like a glove, that he had left in his coat. He kept a small tin of water on top of the stove, to which he added, when he thought of it, coffee, drinking his own from the can but serving Will Brady in a green tin cup. When he stood near the stove the smell of wet gunny sacks steamed out from his clothes. By himself, he spit into the fire, cocking his head like a robin to hear the juice sizzle, but with Will Brady he would walk to the door, spit into the street. The blue knob of his wrist would wipe the brown stain from his lips. Coming back to the stove, he would take off his hat, look carefully into the crown, then use the stub of his arm to hone, tenderly, the soiled brim.

One evening in March, nearly the middle of March, Will Brady stopped the old man at the door to tell him that he could have the next day off. A holiday? Well yes, in a way it was. He, Will Brady, was taking himself another wife. Taking her, he added, before some other lucky fellow did. The old man seemed to think that was pretty sharp, pressing on his mouth to keep his chew in, and Will

Brady pressed a crisp new ten-dollar bill into his one hand. "Have yourself a good time," he said, but perhaps a man who had never had one, never bought one, anyhow, wasn't the man to bring the matter up. The old man stood there with the money, looking at it. Somehow it made Will Brady think of the boy, as when he didn't know what else to do he would give the boy money and say: "Go buy yourself something." The old man stood there, strangely preoccupied. Will Brady left him, but when he looked back he saw that the old man was still in the doorway, but his good arm was stretched across his front to his left side. He was trying to put the money in the pocket where he couldn't take it out. To get it out of that pocket, as he had once said, he had to take his coat off his back, which was not an easy thing for a one-armed man to do. Money put there was usually still there when he needed it.

Will Brady thought of that, oddly enough, when he reached across his front for the girl's small hand, and it may have been why he had a little trouble with the ring. They were married on the second floor of the City Hall. They stood in the anteroom of the Judge's office, facing the Judge himself and the green water-cooler, and the four or five people who were waiting to speak to him. A man who is married for the second time will probably look out the window, if one is handy, and think of the first time that such a thing had happened to him. It seemed, it all seemed, a good while ago. Thinking of that he turned from the window, where a ratty-tailed pigeon was strutting, and looked at the boy —a Western Union boy—who stood in the door. On his way somewhere, the boy had stopped to look in. Perhaps he had never seen a man married before. When he saw Will Brady, and Will Brady saw him, the boy took off his uniform cap, held it at his side, and ran his dirty fingers through his mussy hair. His eyes were wide, his lips were parted, and though there were other people in the room, what you call witnesses, it was only the boy who saw something. It was the boy that reminded Will Brady of what was happening to him. That taking a wife, as he had put it, was a serious affair.

He wanted to go out and speak to the boy, perhaps shake his hand, or give him some money, but all he did, of course, was stand there shaking hands with the Judge. The Judge turned from him to the water-cooler, tipping it forward as it was nearly empty, and had several long drinks from a soiled paper cup. Michael Long, his wife's father, crossed the room to shake Will Brady's hand and give him a wink, showing the gold caps on his teeth. Mr. Long was a dark-haired, rosy-cheeked man who had once been quite an actor, one of the five men, wearing spats, who tried to hide under a bed on the stage. A little old for that now, he had given it up, and come by bus from Kansas City to see the little girl finally hitched—as he said. Mrs. Long herself, a well-preserved woman, was still in considerable demand as the actress who lay in the bed with the men beneath it. This was why she had not been able to come. She was under contract to do three matinees a day.

Michael Long told Will Brady this as they stood in the lobby, but he left the impression with Will Brady that something else, of far greater importance, was on his mind. In the men's room, where they went to think it over, he explained himself. He wanted Will Brady to know, he said—holding his wig flat while he combed it—that he was making no mistake, no sireee, with this little girl. She was just like her mother, he said, who was as good now as she ever was, and by that he meant something better than thirty-five years. Every bit as good, Michael Long said, and put out his hands on something he saw before him, which might have been a stove, a radiator, or a woman's hips.

Mr. Long had told him that before the ceremony, in case he thought he might change his mind, but his hand was still sticky and smelled of hair oil when he shook Will Brady's hand. Will Brady dropped it and wiped his own on the side of his

pants. He kissed an Aunt Lucille, who offered a
cheek like a piece of saddle leather; then he led his
wife down the wrought-iron stairway to the street.
They had left the boy with Mr. Wherry, as he was
a great stickler for details, knew all about wed-
dings, and might object to one in the City Hall. As
they entered the hotel and the smoke-filled lobby,
the girl led him forward to meet the boy as if they
had been lovers, *her* lovers, and now had to patch
up their quarrel.

7

As HIS bride had never been west before, and as
Will Brady wanted her to get the feel of the country, they left Omaha early in the morning on a fine
spring day. Just west of Fremont he took the flapping side curtains off the car. In the West, as he
told her—that is, he told them, as the boy had got
to be quite a city kid—there were no wooded hills
as there were along the river around Council Bluffs.
It was not hilly country, and the rivers were apt to
be wide, shallow affairs, as most of the water was
somewhere underground. It was what men called
open country, where you could see a good ways.
When the sun was right—that is to say, behind you

—a man could see from town to town, and his bride, Gertrude Long, seemed to think that this was wonderful. She was so tired of being cooped up in the dirty city, she said. But when the sun was wrong—as it was when you were driving west, along toward evening—everything that you saw, if you cared to look at it, looked quite a bit alike. Pretty much like the same town, usually, with the same grain elevator along the tracks, and the same gas pump out in front of the same hay and feed store. Through the vibrating windshield, as the roads were pretty bad, the wide empty plain seemed to shimmer, and the telephone poles that slowly crawled past appeared to tremble and blur. The evening sun was like a locomotive headlight in their eyes. To get away from this sun the girl dozed off with her head bumping on Will Brady's shoulder, her mouth open, and her tongue black with the licorice she liked to eat. The boy sprawled with his feet on the seat, his head in her lap. A wad of Black Jack chewing gum was being saved on the bridge of his nose.

Will Brady drove mechanically, his fingers thick like those of the boy when he roller-skated, his hands gripping the wheel, his tired eyes fixed on the road. Once he stopped the car, as he had come to feel that one more mile would rattle him to pieces, but as he sat there, brooding, neither the boy nor the girl woke up. A cow tethered in the field near by turned to gaze at him. Her dung-heavy tail made a flapping sound like that of a loose board, wind-rattled, when it thumped, like a bell clapper, on her hollow frame. He returned her solemn gaze until she started to moo, when he drove on.

A little after sundown he drove into Murdock, an abandoned town on a Sunday evening, with no sign of life anywhere but the revolving barber pole. He drove on through the town, past the piles of cases that were stamped WILL BRADY—EGGS—MURDOCK, and that had been stacked under the shelter, ready for loading, on the station platform. He drove down the road that led, as they said, to the Brady Egg Empire. He had planned it that way, to arrive about sunset, so that the last rays of the sun, no longer touching the plains, might be seen on the tower of the new house. But from the bridge over the creek, which was just a mile or so from the farm, he saw the tower to the house and it struck him as higher than he thought it would be. And the house itself, the bulk of it, struck him as even larger than he had remembered, and a good deal stranger than it had appeared in *Ideal Homes*. Something was missing, but hard to say what it was. It was both larger than he had thought, the tower was higher than he had thought, and somehow or other he had expected a few trees. Perhaps he thought the trees came with the house. There had been a small grove around the house he had seen in the catalogue.

Still it was his own place, all right, as there in the fields were thousands of chickens, and on the new shingled roof were the lightning rods with the polished blue balls. He had asked for them, picked that color out himself. It was their place, but he drove on by, neither slowing down nor honking the horn nor doing anything that he figured might wake his family up.

What if they should ask him who in the world lived in a place like that? What if they should want to know, as they would, who in the world had been such a fool as to build, out here in the country, a fine city house. One that needed a green lawn, many fine big trees with a hammock or two swinging between them, and a birthday party going on clear around the run-around porch. What good was such a house without the city along with it? That's what they would ask him, laughing and hooting when they saw that he had no answer, so he drove on by, neither speaking to them nor shifting the gears. He followed one of the quiet, grass-covered roads back into town. When he drew up at the Cornland Hotel he just sat there for a while, with the motor running, reading the sign that asked guests with horses to leave them in the rear. Then he shut off the motor, and the sudden quiet woke them up.

He left them there in the car, the girl rubbing her eyes, while he stepped up to the counter of the hotel, where a Mr. Riddlemosher, once a neighbor, shook his hand. He asked about the boy as he handed Will Brady the counter pen. He watched Will Brady sign his name, then he twirled the ledger around to read for himself, over his glasses, just what it said. *Will Brady, wife & son.* That was what it said.

"Well," Mr. Riddlemosher said, "well, well—" then he looked up from the ledger to see the boy, his hands full of tinfoil, run into the lobby of the hotel. It was Mr. Riddlemosher who used to buy it from him at ten cents a pound.

8

Ten or twelve hours a day—when he wasn't eating, arguing with his family, or sleeping—Will Brady uncrated the furniture and drove it out to the farm. He had a freight car on the siding, full of it. While he did this he hired a man from Chapman, a farmer with two husky boys, to dig up some small shade trees and plant them in the yard. He wanted *something* to be there in the yard when he drove them out. Something besides chickens, that is, as even the full-grown Leghorn hens looked like so many pillow feathers blowing around a big empty house. They were fine big birds, but they looked awfully small. Everything did.

Now and then he would wake up at night with the notion that his strange house, like a caboose left on a siding, had somehow drifted away during the night. That he would drive out of town in the morning and find it gone. It was a wonderfully hopeful feeling—without it he might not have got up in the morning—but it made it that much worse when he saw that it was still there. Bigger than life. That was the hell of it.

With still half a car of furniture to unload, he had enough sofas for four or five houses, as they would not fit inside of the rooms he had bought them for. The doors opened wrong, or a window proved to be in the way. Some of the beds wouldn't fit in the rooms and he asked Mr. Sykes, his hired hand, if his wife might not care for one of them. What Mrs. Sykes didn't want they stored in the loft of the Sykes barn. It was Mrs. Sykes, of course, who asked him, when he came to the door of the kitchen, when he was going to get around to the kitchen stove. An honest man, Will Brady simply said he hadn't thought of it.

In the Clearing

It seemed hard to believe, a little weird in fact, that a man like Will Brady, born and raised in a soddy, had spent three thousand dollars without buying himself a kitchen stove. Had he come up too fast? Mrs. Sykes implied as much. She stood there looking at him, then said: "Well, it's up to the woman to think of the stove," and maybe it was. But not every woman. Not one like his wife.

He tried to explain, as they drove into town, that the reason his wife hadn't thought of the stove was that city-born girls, of a certain type, never cooked anything. They ate in restaurants. The food they ate was brought to them.

And who, Mrs. Sykes said, was going to bring her food to her in the country?

Well, that was one more thing he hadn't got around to thinking about. There had been too many things. There had also been restaurants where they could eat.

But he thought of that, among other things, as he watched Mrs. Sykes build a fire in the stove, breaking the stiff pine kindling between her strong hands and over her knee. Tough pieces she leaned on the leg of the stove, then stepped on them. She set the drafts on the pipes, then dipped a corncob into a pail of kerosene, lit it with a match, and used it like a torch to start the fire. As it roared up the chimney she said: "Well, I guess it draws all right."

111

Mrs. Sykes was an angular woman, a little blunt in her ways, and Will Brady felt right at home with her, as his own family treated him the same way. As a man, that is, who didn't seem to know anything. Not only in the woman's place, in the kitchen, but if Mrs. Sykes saw him out in the yard she would call to him, put a pail or a shovel into his hand. On a farm, she told him, something always needed to be done.

Would she happen to know a woman, he said, who would like a nice home in the country? A woman like herself, who would like to do the cooking, look after the house.

Mrs. Sykes wiped her hands and stiffened her back at the same time. She held her right hand to her face˙and picked at a splinter in the palm.

Did he know what it was like, she said, to keep a thirteen-room house?

Suppose they just closed off some of the upstairs rooms, he said. Would a woman like herself mind keeping a five- or six-room house?

Did he think, she replied, a woman would call that *keeping house*? That was what she said, leaving him there in the empty kitchen, with the fire burning, and the smell of the paint rising from the new stove. Then she was back—her head in the door but her face turned away from him. She said that she did know a woman, and if she happened to see her she might bring it up. But she wouldn't recommend it to any woman—not something like that. Then the door slammed behind her in a way that made it clear what she thought.

Four or five days later, a Saturday morning, Will Brady thought he saw Mrs. Sykes in the kitchen, but the woman who turned to face him had white hair. She was panning water from the bin on the range, the handle of the pan wrapped in her apron, and he had the feeling that she might be a little deaf. She didn't seem to be surprised to see him standing there. A tall heavy-bodied woman, with a dark skin, she didn't look any too well around the eyes, but to see her working, it was clear that she was strong enough.

"You're from Mrs. Sykes?" he said to her, raising his voice as she didn't seem to hear him. She stooped for some cobs, then settled the kettle over the plate hole.

"Mrs. Sykes said you could use a woman," she said.

"My wife is a city-bred girl," he said, which was true enough, but strange to hear him say it. "And city girls," he went on, "aren't really used to country ways."

That was strange kind of talk for him, but the woman seemed to follow it. It didn't seem to strike her, as it did Mrs. Sykes, that a city-bred girl was out of place in the country.

"To tell you the simple truth," he said, as he felt an urge to speak on this topic, "I suppose what I've tried to do is to bring the city out here." He gestured with his arm at the house, then added, "I wanted her to feel at home out here." Nor did this woman seem to see anything strange in that. "My name is Will Brady," he said, "and I'm very glad you've come to help us out. If the house is too big—" he waved his hand at the house, "we can shut some of it off."

"I'm getting on now," this woman said, "but I can still keep a house."

She didn't seem to feel it necessary to say any more than that. He stood there, and after a moment he realized that the sound that he heard, like a pole humming, was one that she made in her throat. A familiar hymn. She was humming it.

"If there's anything I can do," he said, "I want you to feel free to call on me." Then he coughed, took a drink of water, and hurried out. Where had he picked up such a fancy way of putting things? He turned back to the door and said: "If you want anything, let me know," but she seemed to be busy again and had her back to him. He crossed the yard to Mr. Sykes, who was mixing up a barrel of laying mash, but he stopped when Will Brady walked up to him.

"You happen to know this old lady's name?" he asked.

"Mason," Mr. Sykes said. "Anna Mason—she's a good sort."

"She strikes me as a pretty fine woman," Will Brady said.

"She's a good sort," Sykes said again.

But there was something about the woman that Will Brady felt needed some comment. "I'd say she was a woman a man could depend on," he said.

"Kept house for her brother," Sykes said, "going on about forty years. He died last year. Guess she misses him."

"She never married?" Will Brady asked.

"No, she never married," Sykes said; then he looked up and said: "She had her brother, one of her own people, to think of."

In April it was spring out in the yard, where the fat hens made nests in the dust heaps, but the winter still seemed to be trapped in the house. Mrs. Sykes had finally told him about the stove, but nobody had told him about the furnace, which was supposed to have been in the basement of the house. Now that the house was up, there was no longer any way of getting it there. The basement was a big whitewashed room, clean-smelling from the earth, and sometimes even sunny, so he put his desk in the basement and lived down there himself. It was handy to the yard, and getting in and out he didn't trouble anyone.

The boy and girl—that was what he called them —lived, with an oil stove, in the master bedroom on the second floor, where they had their meals unless he drove them into town to eat. During the day they played phonograph records on the machine he had ordered from Omaha, and when the windows were up he could often hear the music himself. The kind of music that they liked sounded very strange in the chicken yard.

Although there was always work to do, and not enough help on the place to do it, he sometimes found himself at the narrow basement windows, peering out. The window on the yard was about chest-high, with a deep sill that he could lean on, and he found that he could see out without Mrs. Sykes being able to see in. Twice a day the local train came down from the north, and even before the bell was ringing, Will Brady would be there at the window, peering out. He liked to watch the smoke pouring from the wide funnel stack. As she came around the curve, the bell wagging, the fireman would climb out of the cab and crawl back over the coal car to the water bin. She took water in Murdock, and he had to be there to pull the stack down. Will Brady would look on while all of this happened, seeing very little from where he stood, but knowing, as an old railroad man, what was taking place. He could hear, on certain days, the water pouring through the chute. He might be able to see a passenger or two get on or off. And all this time the bell would be ringing as there were no guard gates on the Burlington crossing, nothing but kids who would be standing on the cowcatcher, waiting for the brakeman to run up front and shoo them off.

Will Brady would stand there, maybe five or ten minutes, until the caboose finally disappeared, and he could hear the whistle, thin and wild, as if the train was calling for help. Was something wrong with him? Or was it just spring fever, or something like that. A tendency to let the team idle on the bridge, so that he could see, through the cracks, the clear water, or to let them graze in the sweet grass at the side of the road. Only flipping the reins now and then to keep the flies off their spanky rumps.

After several years of working day and night, perhaps Will Brady had begun to stop working, to stand as if thinking, as if great thoughts were troubling his mind. Mr. Sykes often had to repeat everything he said. It was not the proper state of

mind for a man who had around five thousand laying hens to think of, and who had often been asked
what he intended to do when one hen took sick.
Well, he didn't know. No, he didn't even know
that. Standing at the basement window he sometimes marveled at this strange fellow, Will Jennings
Brady, known all over the state as an up and coming man of caliber. A man who lived in the basement of his fine new thirteen-room house.

On a Sunday morning, on his way into town, he
found this woman Anna Mason walking down the
road, her skirts pinned up, and her long underwear
tucked into her high laced shoes. When he stopped
and spoke to her she said she was on her way to
church. A woman nearly seventy years of age,
heavy on her feet and not any too well, on her way
to a church that was a good three-mile walk.

"Now look here," he said, but she wouldn't listen to him. Nor would she get into the car and ride
in with him. She would go to church, she let him
know, just so long as she could get there; when
she couldn't get there any more, why, then she
wouldn't go. She would be dead then, she said, and
looked at him.

All right, he replied, but he would be there to
bring her home.

If he just happened to be there in the church,

she said, if he happened to be there, and she happened to see him, why, then she supposed he might as well bring her home.

He wondered if that was how it happened that most men went to church. There would be a woman there, too old to walk, who would like a ride home. A woman with white or gray hair, her long underwear tucked into her shoe tops, and spectacles that had got to be the color of flecked isinglass. She would be there in the pew, her hands in her lap, or pushing up to share with somebody her hymnbook, then singing, or humming, in a voice that made little boys wet their pants. He had done just that, anyway, many times. His mother had had such a voice, throbbing like an organ on the chorus, and this throb passed down through her arm into his hand, the one she was holding, and made the small hairs rise on his neck, and his knees rub. And when the hymn was over he usually found that his pants were wet.

Now he came late and took a seat near the door, where he had sat that Sunday that the boy had won a Bible, with his name stamped on it, and brought it up the aisle to him. Where, come to think of it, was that Bible now? He had driven them all—it was Ethel then—out to Nolan's Lake for the barbecue, the motorboat ride, and the hymn-singing after dark. The choir in their long white robes on the platform, the hissing red flares very good on the women, and in the dark like that, out in the open, he could sing himself. It was said that he had a fine baritone voice. Well, that night he had sung many hymns, the fires had made it seem like a gypsy encampment, and the boy, who had eaten too much, fell asleep in his lap. The new Bible, with the cover sticky, had dropped from his hand. Will Brady had picked it up and said: "Ethel, maybe you better take that Bible," and she had said yes, and that was the last he saw of it. Moving around, as they did, it was hard to keep track of things.

From where he sat at the back, beneath the limp flags, and with the stack of collection plates beside him, he thought he could pick out Anna Mason's voice. Anna Mason would have his mother's voice, and with it his mother's kind of religion, and a man with his voice, and his kind of religion, was not in her class. He didn't belong, if the truth were known, in the same church. But he was there now, he was sure, for a good Christian reason, and he had something like a religious feeling about the choir. They wore black gowns and sat under the golden organ pipes. They rose as one, the women at the front and the men, who were taller, lined up in back, and the sound of their robes was like the clearing of one great throat. They sang, and he closed his eyes and waited for the moment when they would stop and there would be nothing, nothing—till the first hymnbook closed. That moment always struck him as something like a prayer. He observed it, that is, as he did Memorial Day, and in that sense of the word he considered himself a religious man.

Then he would stand by the aisle, his hat in his hand, until Anna Mason came up and walked by him, and he would not step to her side until she reached the street. She was not a woman to stand out in front and talk with someone. But she did think it was pleasant to take a short buggy ride. Not in the car, which made her nervous—as she liked the horses out in front, where she could see them, not bottled up, like some sort of genie, under the hood. She liked it off the paving, along the streets where the buggy wheels ran quiet in the dust, and the reins made a soft, lapping sound on the rumps of the mares. As it just happened to be on their way, they usually passed the house where the blinds were drawn, and there were still three birches, a little larger now, there in the yard. He admitted to her that he had owned that house. He said owned advisedly, as the words *lived in* struck him as strange, and did not describe, as he remembered, what he had done in the house. But for several years he had come back and gone to bed there. It was in that house he had had erysipelas, a painful, contagious disease, and a woman, his wife at the time, had taken care of him. Lovingly, as the doctor had said. A very strange word, he thought, and he had marveled at it. She had made him well, she had kept him clean, and when he was fit to be seen again, he had made love to a plump cigar-counter girl. How was that? Time passed. Perhaps that was it. Every morning it was there on his hands, and had to be passed.

But if it was Anna Mason that got him to church, and kept him there while the choir was singing, it was a chicken—a sick chicken—that made him a religious man. It made a man wonder, and wonder makes a religious man. Some people might say that it was the girl, or the city house he had built out in the country, but he knew in his heart it was neither the house nor his family. It was the chicken. Nobody needed to tell him that.

Now, a sick chicken is always a problem, but when you put that chicken with five thousand others, all of them Leghorns, your problem is out of hand. The people in Murdock, you might say, had figured on that. They had all looked forward to it, and some men put their families into buggies and drove them out in the country so they could watch Will Brady's chickens die. All day long he could hear the buggy weights plop in the dust. Just by turning and looking at the buggies he could tell which way the wind was blowing, as they were always careful to park away from the smell. Others claimed they could smell it clear in town. He never knew, personally, as he never got out of the yard, and he slept in the basement where Anna Mason brought him his food. He couldn't have smelled very much anyhow, as he was covered with smells from head to foot, and dirty Leghorn feathers were said to be tangled in his hair. Even Anna Mason, a pioneer woman, kept out of his draft.

In the second week the big hens were dead before he picked them up. It was not necessary to cut their throats or to wring their necks. They were stiff, and yet they seemed very light when he scooped them up on the shovel, as if dying had taken a load off of them. During the third week three experts arrived, at his expense, from Chicago, and took most of one day to tell him there was nothing to be done. Then they went off, after carefully washing their hands.

Sometimes he stopped long enough to look out at the road, and the rows of buggies, where the women and the kids sat breathing through their handkerchiefs. That was something they had picked up during the war. When the flu came along, everyone had run around breathing through a handkerchief. In spite of the smell, they all liked to sit where they could keep their eyes on the house, and the upstairs room where the boy and girl were in quarantine. He had more or less ordered them to stay inside. Now and then he caught sight of the boy with his head at the window, peering at him, and one evening he thought he heard, blown to him, the music of their phonograph. Something about a lover who went away and did not come back.

Nothing that he did, or paid to have done, seemed to help. The hens he shipped off died on the railroad platform overnight. They were left in their crates and shipped back to him for burial. He was advised to keep his sick chickens to himself. Other men had chickens, and what he had started might sweep across the state, across the nation, right at the time that the state and the nation were doing pretty well.

And then it stopped—for no more apparent reason than it had begun. It left him with one hundred and twenty-seven pullets still alive. He sat around waiting for them to die, but somehow they went on living, they even grew fatter, and early every morning the three young roosters crowed. It was something like the first, and the last, sound that he had ever heard. When he heard them crow he would come to the window, facing the cold morning sky, and look at the young trees that he had planted at the edge of the yard. They were wired to the ground, which kept them, it was said, from blowing away.

It would soon be summer out in the yard, but when he went up the spiralling stairs to their room, he could smell the oil burner that they kept going day and night. They liked the smell of it better than the one out in the yard. There was music playing, and when he opened the door a man's clear voice, as if right there before him, came out of the horn that had the picture of the white dog stamped on it. The boy, the girl, and the dog were all listening to him. The man was singing of the time when the girl was a tulip, and he was a rose. This had been, he seemed to remember, her favorite song. As the man went on singing, the girl took hold of his hand, looking toward the horn where the needle was scratching, and he saw that she had no idea of what had happened to him. Not an inkling. Nor had the boy, who was sniffling through his adenoids. They had lived in this private world together, playing their records, caroms, and dominoes, and sometimes marveling at the strange things they saw in the yard. It seemed hard to believe, but somehow it didn't trouble him. When the music stopped he heard her say: "Will, you remember?"

"Why, yes," he said, his head nodding, and put a warm smile on his face. And when they both looked at him, waiting, he knew what he would say. He had come into the room not knowing, not having the vaguest idea, but now he knew, and he looked through the window as he spoke to them.

"How would you two like to go to Omaha?" he said.

IN THE MOONLIGHT

1

IN THE middle of life Will Brady bought a house with the roof on sideways, as the boy said, and a yard without grass that he could pay the boy to mow. Under the fenced-in porch were a lawnmower and a cracked garden hose. On the porch were a swing, a hammock rope, and between the stone pillars at the front two wire baskets of dead ferns. In the house were a new player piano and a large box of music rolls.

From the swing on the porch, since the ferns were dead, Will Brady could look down the street to the park, the end of the car line, and the health-giving mineral spring. At night, when the motorman changed the trolley, there would be a hot sizzling sound, and flashes of white light, like heat lightning, would fill the air. From where he sat on the porch Will Brady could see that the ferns were dead.

Beyond the mineral spring, said to be good for you, the green hills were trimmed by mowing machines, and men could be seen playing the new game of golf. They wore breeches quite a bit like those worn by the boy. The hitting of the ball took place near the spring, where the men would stop for a drink of the water while the boys went off with the bags of sticks to hunt for the ball. Will Brady bought the boy a set of the sticks, which he found around the front yard every evening, and a box of the balls, which he often heard rolling around the house. He couldn't seem to interest either the boy or the girl in the park. It was too big, too open, and too much like Murdock, they said.

Sunday afternoons, to be with his family, he would sit in the parlor with the player piano while the boy played some of the rolls backwards, others too fast. The girl would sit on the floor playing card games with herself. On the table at his side were the magazines, the *Youth's Companion* and *Boys' Life*, that came through the mail once a month for the boy to read. He read them himself, and ordered through the mail such things as the watch with the compass in the winder, and the Official Scout knife, with which a clever boy could do so many things. One of the watches he bought for the boy, the other for himself. In the dark candling-room he liked to take it from his pocket and watch the tiny needle waver toward the north, telling him, as nothing else would, about where he was.

On top of the magazines, perhaps to keep them from blowing, was a heavy glass ball with a castle inside, and when he took this ball and shook it, the castle would disappear. Quite a bit the way a farmhouse on the plains would disappear in a storm. He liked to sit there, holding this ball, until the storm had passed, the sky would clear, and he would see that the fairy castle with the waving red flags was still there.

Every morning, with the exception of Sunday, Will Brady would get out of bed at six thirty, fry himself two eggs, and eat them while standing on the fenced-in back porch, facing the yard. At that time in the morning a rabbit might be there. He would then leave some money on the kitchen table and drive through the town to his place of work, a long narrow building with a wooden awning out in front. As the owner of this business he wore a soiled jacket, with blue flaps on the pockets, and when he stood in the door there was usually a clipboard on his arm. On it he kept a record of the eggs that came in, the chickens that went out. He also wore a green visor and a sober preoccupied air. In the middle of life, with his best years before him, he seemed to have a firm grip on all serious matters, and a pretty young wife who called him once a day on the telephone. She called to let her husband know what movie his wife and son were at.

In the morning there was usually ice on the pail where the dung-spotted eggs were floating, and he could see his breath, as if he were smoking, in the candling-room. If he seemed to spend a good deal of time every day looking at one egg and scratching another, perhaps it was the price one had to pay for being a successful man. One whose life was still before him, but so much of it already behind him that it seemed that several lives—if that was the word for it—had already been lived. Had already gone into the limbo, as some men said.

He had his noon meal across the street, usually chicken-fried steak and hash-brown potatoes, or stuffed baked heart with a piece of banana cream pie. After eating this meal he would stand on the curbing out in front. As he neither smoked anything nor chewed, he would usually stand there chewing on a toothpick, and he seemed to have the time to listen to what you had to say. He seldom interrupted to say anything himself. He neither heard anything worth recounting nor said anything worth repeating, but he gave strangers the feeling that one of these days he might. He was highly respected and said to be wise in the ways of the world.

There were evenings that he sat at the desk in the office, with the Dun & Bradstreet open before him, and there were other evenings that he spent in the candling-room. He would take a seat on one of his egg cases, using the thick excelsior pad as a cushion, and the light from the candler would fall on the book he held in his hands. Dun & Bradstreet? No, this book was called a *Journey to the Moon*. Written by a foreigner who seemed to have been there. Will Brady's son had read this book, and then he had given it to his father, as he did all of his books, to return to the library. One day Will Brady wondered what it was the boy liked to read. So he had opened the book, read four or five pages himself. He had been standing there, at his candler, but after reading a few more pages he had seated himself on an egg case, adjusted the light. He had gone without his lunch, without food or drink, till he had finished it. The candling-room had turned cold, and when he stepped into the office it was dark outside.

That night Will Brady had tried to sleep—that is to say, he went to bed as usual—but something about having been to the moon kept him awake. He got out of the bed and stepped out on the porch for a look at it. The moon that he saw looked larger than usual, and nearer at hand. And the light from this moon cast a different light on the neighborhood. There before him lay the city—growing, it was said, by leaps and bounds since the last census —where many thousands of men, with no thought of the moon, lay asleep. He could cope with the moon, but somehow he couldn't cope with a thought like that. It seemed a curious arrangement, he felt, for God to make. By some foolish agreement, made long ago, men and women went into their houses and slept, or tried to sleep, right when there was the most to see.

Over the sleeping city the moon was rising, and there in the street were the shady elms, the flowering shrubs, and the sidewalks slippery with maple pods. On the porches were swings, limp, sagging hammocks, roller skates, and wire baskets of ferns, and in the houses the men and women lay asleep. It all seemed to Will Brady, there in the moonlight, a very strange thing. A warm summer night, the windows and the doors of most of the houses were open, and the air that he breathed went in and out of all of them. In and out of the lungs, and the lives, of the people who were asleep. They inhaled it deeply, snoring perhaps; then they blew it on its way again, and he seemed to feel himself sucked into the rooms, blown out again. Without carrying things too far, he felt himself made part of the lives

134

of these people, even part of the dreams that they were having, lying there. Was that a very strange thing? Well, perhaps it was. Perhaps it was stranger, even, than a Journey to the Moon.

And the thought came to him—to Will Jennings Brady, a prominent dealer in eggs—that he was a traveler, something of an explorer, himself. That he did even stranger things than the men in books. It was one thing to go to the moon, like this foreigner, a writer of books, but did this man know the man or the woman across the street? Had he ever traveled into the neighbor's house? Did he know the woman who was there by the lamp, or the man sitting there in the shadow, a hat on his head as if at any moment he might go out? Could he explain why there were grass stains on the man's pants? That might be stranger, that might be harder to see, than the dark side of the moon.

Perhaps it was farther across the street, into that room where the lamp was burning, than it was to the moon, around the moon, and back to the earth. Where was there a traveler to take a voyage like that? Perhaps it was even farther than twenty thousand leagues under the sea. Men had been there, it was said, and made a thorough report of the matter, but where was the man who had traveled the length of his own house? Who knew the woman at the back—or the boy at the front who lay asleep?

How many moons away, how many worlds away, was a boy like that? On the moon a man might jump many feet, which might be interesting if you went there; but it was no mystery, a man could explain something like that. But what about the man who stood in the dark eating cornbread and milk? What about the rooms where the blinds were always drawn? If there were men who had been there and knew the answers, he would like to know them; if they had written about these things he would read the book. If they hadn't, perhaps he would write such a book himself.

What writer, what traveler, could explain the woman who rolled herself up in the sheet, like a mummy, or the man who came home every night and undressed in the dark? All one could say was that whatever it was it was there in the house, like a vapor, and it had drawn the blinds, like an invisible hand, when the lights came on. As a writer of books he would have to say that this vapor made the people yellow in color, gave them flabby bodies, and made their minds inert. As if they were poisoned, all of them, by the air they breathed. And such a writer would have to explain why this same air, so fresh and pure in the street, seemed to be poisoned by the people breathing it. So that in a way even stranger than the moon, they poisoned themselves.

In the Moonlight

Was it any wonder that men wrote books about other things? That they traveled to the moon, so to speak, to get away from themselves? Were they all nearer to the moon, the bottom of the sea, and such strange places than they were to their neighbors, or the woman there in the house? What the world needed, it seemed, was a traveler who would stay right there in the bedroom, or open the door and walk slowly about his own house. Who would sound a note, perhaps, on the piano, raise the blinds on the front-room windows, and walk with a candle into the room where the woman sleeps. A man who would recognize this woman, this stranger, as his wife.

But if books would put a man in touch with the moon, perhaps they would put him in touch with a boy—a very strange thing, but a lot of people owned up to them. Mothers and fathers alike seemed to be familiar with them. When he returned the *Journey to the Moon*, he spoke to Mrs. Giles, the librarian, and tried to phrase, for her, some of the thoughts that were troubling him. Had any man taken, he said, a journey around his own house?

Not for public perusal, Mrs. Giles said.

That would be a journey, he said, that he would like to take, or, for that matter, a journey around his own son.

That had been done, Mrs. Giles said, so he could just save himself the trouble. All kinds of men had already done just that.

Was that a fact? he said.

Hadn't he read *Tom Sawyer*? she said.

And who was Tom Sawyer? he said, so she brought him the book. She also brought him *Penrod,* by another man, and several books by Ralph Henry Barbour, that would give him a good idea, she said, of what was on a boy's mind. That was just what he wanted to know, he said, and went off with the books.

He read *Tom Sawyer*, in one sitting, in the candling-room. He took the tin bottom off the candler, so that it cast more light for him, and he used two of the excelsior egg pads to soften the seat. There was a much better light in the office, with a comfortable chair to sit in, but he had hired a girl to sit there at the desk and answer telephone calls. She might not understand a man of his age reading children's books.

He read *Tom Sawyer* during the morning, and reflected on it while he had his lunch; then he came back and read the book by Tarkington. By supper time a great load had been lifted from his mind. If he could believe what he read—which he found hard, but not too hard if he put his mind to it—boys were not at all as complicated as he had been led to believe. When all was said and done, so to speak, they were just boys. Full of boyish devilment and good clean fun. If neither this Penrod nor Tom Sawyer reminded him very much of Willy Brady, that might be explained in terms of how they lived. Penrod had brothers and sisters, many freckles and friends, and a very loving father and mother. Willy Brady didn't have all of these things. But if his father could believe what he read, all Willy Brady had on his mind was baseball, football, Honor, and something called track. In Ralph Henry Barbour's opinion, that of a man who really seemed to know, these were the things at the front and the back of a boy's mind. If he could believe what he read, and Will Brady did, it was coming from behind in the great mile race that made the difference between a boy and a man. But to lead all the way was to court disaster, as the book made clear.

One began with a fine healthy boy like Penrod, who had a real home, a loving father and mother, and perhaps an older sister who brought out the best in him. Then one day, overnight almost, his voice would change. Fuzz would grow on his lip, and his father would send him off to a boarding school. There he would live with other clean-cut boys like himself, eating good food, reading fine books, and talking over the problems of the coming Oglethorpe game. The walls of the room would be covered with banners from big Eastern schools. The window would open out on the field where he would throw the javelin, run the race, and pitch the last three innings with a pain in his arm. In the winter he would sit at his desk and study, or go home with his roommate over Christmas, whose father was a big corporation lawyer of some kind. His roommate's sister, a dark-haired girl who attended some private school in the East, would ask her brother, in a roundabout way, all about him. After that one thing would lead to another until he struck off somewhere on his own, or accepted a position with a promising future in her father's firm. The only problem would be how long he would have to wait for her.

Will Brady hoped it wouldn't be too long, thinking over his own experience, as once out of school, like that, life seemed harder to organize. There were many pressures, and not nearly so many lovely girls. Nor were there many things that a father could do to make sure that the boy picked the right one, when the boy still had neither fuzz on his lip nor a voice that had changed. He was twelve, but he looked more like nine or ten. The only hair on his body was there on the top of his head. But with this boy he did what he could—that is to say, on Sundays afternoons he would walk him through the park to the baseball diamond, and sit with him in the bleachers behind the sagging fence of chicken wire. Thanks to Ralph Henry Barbour, Will Brady knew the names of the players and the places, and he pointed out to the boy the pitcher's mound, and the batteries. In his own mind, of course, he saw the boy as a pitcher, pitching the last three innings with his arm sore, but the boy took an interest in the catcher as he wanted the mask. Nobody else on the field seemed to interest him. He wanted to wear what the catcher wore, and peer out through the mask. So he bought the boy a glove, a ball, and a mask, but he put off buying the rest of it until he had a long talk with the man in the Spalding store. This man, a Mr. Lockwood, seemed to take a personal interest in Will Brady's boy.

Mr. Lockwood had been a great athlete himself. As a student at the University of Nebraska he had run the mile in record time, the last thing you would think of, so to speak, when you looked at him. He didn't look any too well, as a matter of fact, and he had grown a little heavy for a man his age. In a separate compartment of his wallet, however, Mr. Lockwood had a bundle of press clippings, some of them with faded pictures showing how he looked at the time. The clippings were now yellow, and hard to read, but Will Brady could make out that the man who stood before him had once run the mile, all the way, in 4:23. A mile, as Mr. Lockwood reminded him, was fourteen city blocks.

With Mr. Lockwood's expert help, Will Brady bought the boy shoes for running and jumping, shoes for baseball, special shoes for football, and rubber-soled shoes for doing things inside. He also bought him the shirts, pants, and socks to go along with all of these things. He might grow out of them at any time, but he would know the smell and the feel of a sweatshirt, and the smell was an important thing. As Mr. Lockwood said, it was a smell that he would never get out of his nose.

If there was something about Mr. Lockwood that had gone unmentioned in all of the books, perhaps it was because the author had had no need to bring it up. As a writer of books, Ralph Henry Barbour described what he saw in the newspaper clippings, and the young man that he saw, with his muscles bulging, breasting the tape. He was not concerned with the middle-aged man in the sporting-goods store. Everything Mr. Lockwood said about himself, and his wonderful college life at Nebraska, would lead one to believe that Ralph Henry Barbour was absolutely right. Everything that had happened to him, back then, had been wonderful. If he had been a writer, he would have written those books himself. Listening to Mr. Lockwood, and he

liked to talk, Will Brady often came away with
the feeling that Ralph Henry Barbour had given
a modest picture of college life. Everything in the
world, it seemed clear, had happened to Mr. Lockwood, the great mile runner, but nothing much
had happened to the man in the sporting-goods
store. Nothing much had happened since then,
that is. He still had the smell of it all in his nose,
and some people might say there was something
like it, if not worse, on his breath. He reminded
Will Brady, at times, of a man very much like
himself. A man who might live in one of those
houses across the street. He would probably have
a wife named Gladys, who slept alone in the bedroom at the back, and a daughter named Mabel, or
Eileen, who slept in the room at the front. And
perhaps at this point people were saying how much
the mother looked like the daughter, and talk like
that would be scaring the girl to death. Or maybe it
wouldn't. That would be hard to say. Perhaps it
was her father she took after, having his light-
brown hair, his pale-blue eyes, and perhaps the
smile that he once had in the photographs. Before
he began to die, that is. Before something began to
poison him.

It was no help, of course, to say so, but the man
in the sporting-goods store, the celebrated athlete,
looked like a man who was being poisoned to death.

He smoked too much. Perhaps that was it. The man who was pictured in the press clippings did not smoke. Whatever this thing was, it seemed to be something that he had picked up later; it was not in the air on the college campus, nor what he breathed on the track. It was not something that Ralph Henry Barbour felt he had to describe. But something had happened. What had it been? The great mile runner, the baseball star, had accepted an offer from Spalding & Brothers to go out on the road and sell their guaranteed baseballs, their autographed bats. After a while he had married his childhood sweetheart, settled down. For a year or two he had kept his paper clippings just loose in his desk, where he could find them; then one day, one spring day more than likely, he took them out. After mulling them over he put them in his wallet —began to carry them around. Some time later maybe he noticed how dry and brittle they were getting, or maybe he didn't—maybe it was just a chance remark by his wife. Whatever it was, he made a little pile of the best of them. He put the best picture in the back of his watch, the best clipping in his vest. They were always with him, as if he couldn't part with them. Some writer of books might even say that these clippings poisoned him. That they were old, brittle, and fading, like the man himself. People will believe anything that they

read, and if they happened to read, in a book somewhere, that a man was poisoned by some newspaper
clippings, why they would swallow it. And a writer
of books might even say that these people were
right.

But what would this man say of Will Brady's
son? One that happened to be, as Will Brady
seemed to think, the complicated type. A boy that
once a week, while his father was shaving, would
come to the door of the bathroom and wait for his
father to turn from the mirror and look at him.
The boy would be wearing his Official Boy Scout
uniform. He seemed to wear the shirt more than
the pants, as the shirt had faded to a washed-out
color, and on his feet were the Official green,
chrome leather shoes. They hurt his feet, badly,
but he never complained. From his belt hung a
flashlight, a compass, a metal canteen in a soft flannel cooler, a key ring with some keys, a medal for
swimming, another medal for walking, one for not
smoking, and a waterproof kit containing materials
for building a fire. This was in case his waterproof
matchbox got wet. On his back was a knapsack
containing maps, a snake-bite cure, a day's balanced
rations, and Dentyne gum, which he chewed for
his teeth and to allay the thirst.

"Off for the woods, son?" Will Brady would say,

145

but sometimes the boy wasn't. No, strange to say, he might not be off for anywhere. He would just be prepared, in case he felt like being off. He would follow his father back to the bedroom and sit on the bed. He would sit there and watch his father dress, as if there was something very strange about it, or he would take out his maps and spread them on the bed.

"Where is the exact center of the U. S. A.?" the boy might ask. At one time Will Brady thought such a question was put to him. He didn't answer for the simple reason that he didn't know. But the boy was just talking to himself, as first he would put the question, then he would answer: "The geographical center of the United States is in Osborne County, Kansas." It was never necessary for Will Brady to say anything. Looking at Omaha the boy would say: "The metal smokestack at the smelting works is the highest metal smokestack in the world," or "Omaha spaghetti is now sold in Italy."

It was something of an education for Will Brady to listen to him. They seemed to be educating young people better nowadays. As for himself, he had eight years' schooling, but in so far as he could remember, no one had ever mentioned that Omaha spaghetti was sold in Italy. The boy said it was. And he always seemed to have the Gospel truth.

Right out of the blue, without any warning, the

boy once asked: "Why are you so different?" Will Brady had been facing the mirror in the men's room of the Paxton Hotel. He had taken the boy down there before they went to the show.

"Kid—" he had said, then hearing what he had said he turned the water on, let it run. After a bit he turned it off and said: "Yes, son?"

"I don't mind kid," the boy said, "if you want to call me kid that's all right with me."

"That was a slip, son," he said. "That was just a slip."

"The name I really like is Spud," the boy said. "I always say call me Spud but nobody does it."

"What's wrong with Willy, son?" he said.

"I've been Willy for a long time," the boy said, and Will Brady bent over, turned the hot water back on. What in God's name did the boy mean by that? With a paper towel Will Brady wiped the steaming mirror so that he could see the boy's sober face. His eyes, his mother's eyes, that is, were watching him. What did Will Brady feel? Not much of anything.

"All right, kid," he said, and that was just about that.

He would take them out to eat, where music was playing, and they would sit there together, in league against him, looking at him from a long way off. Very much as if he were an imposter. A father, one who didn't know what being a father was like, and a lover, one who didn't know much about love. More or less hopeless. For different reasons they both pitied him.

2

So HE would give them money, put them in a show, and drive downtown to his office, where he would take off his coat and sit at his new roll-top desk.

Some nights he did that, other nights he might walk around the streets, or out over the river, and on Saturday evenings he often stopped in at Browning King. It was Fred Conlen who had got him to wear the soft-collar shirt. In Fred Conlen's private fitting-room he would see himself in the three-way mirror, and it was there that he saw the new expression on his face. While he was talking— at no other time. While he talked this man in the mirror had a strange smile on his lips. This smile on his lips and a sly, knowing look about the eyes. Something shrewd he had said? Well, he never really seemed to say much. Just a good deal implied, so to speak, in what he did say.

"What about a pair of pants," he would say, "that a man never has to take off?" That was all.

What did he mean by a remark like that? Whatever he meant, Fred Conlen often thought it was pretty good.

"Brady," he would say, "you ought to be on the platform. You got a head."

"When I was a boy," Will Brady had said, "I had the biggest hat on the lowest peg. Seems to me the peg's lower every time I look at it."

"Bygod, Brady," Fred Conlen had said, "there you said something."

Had he? Well, nothing you could put your finger on. You needed mirrors, so to speak, to see a trick like that. To see a man with a big head, narrow shoulders, the new soft-collared shirt, and along with the toothpick that sly smile in the corner of his mouth. About to say something. And when he did, it would be pretty good.

"I notice these new twin beds are pretty popular now," he would say, and Fred Conlen, with the pins in his mouth, would turn to look at him.

Will Brady bought his clothes from Fred Conlen —Hart Schaffner & Marx, direct from Chicago— and his shoes from Lyman Bryce, who ran the Florsheim store. If he stopped by in the evening Lyman Bryce would take him to the back of the shop, pull up a stool, and show him what they were wearing in Palm Beach. Will Brady would sit there, his shoes off, and this fellow Bryce, a gray-haired man, would lace him into the latest thing in Palm Beach shoes. He would ask him to stand up and walk around in them. People in the street would come to the door and peer in. Bryce had a fine new home in Dundee, and a prominent place in the Ak-Sar-Ben parade, but what he really liked to do was sit there on a shoe stool and talk. He was a big fellow, like T. P. Luckett, but he was quite a bit different from Luckett in that he hinted that a good egg business was not the last word. Nor was the shoe business. Nor anything of that stripe. Lyman Bryce seemed to think that Will Brady was meant for more than that. "Forget about the money," Bryce would say, "I'll take care of the money." What he seemed to be looking for, as he said himself, was the right man.

What was being done, Bryce wanted to know, down in the deep South, or out in Texas? Wouldn't a little loose money start something really rolling out there? Couldn't a man with a few big tractors start plowing it up? Instead of fiddling with eggs—as Bryce called it—why didn't Will Brady take thirty thousand dollars, or fifty if he liked it, and go out there and start something? "God Almighty, Brady," he would say, "stop fiddling with eggs." He seemed to think the country was still wide open for a man with some cash.

In the Moonlight

When he talked with Lyman Bryce, Will Brady always had a smile on his face. Was he amused? No, there was more to his smile than that. It was more like the smile he had when he faced three mirrors with just one face. Or when he sat there with Bryce, and Bryce would say: "Now bygod, Brady, I'd like to have you home for dinner. But you know the little woman—the little woman is fussy as hell."

Did he know *the little woman?* From that smile on his face, you would think that he did. You might be led to think that some of these little women were pretty big.

Clark Lee, for example, had one of them. Lee ran the Gaiety, and he was one of the big show men in the state. He used *the little woman* to explain a good many things. "Geez, Brady," he would say, "I wouldn't want the little woman to get wind of this," or "Well, I'd better get along, Brady, if I'm going to keep the little woman in line." Now, both Lee and Bryce were pretty big men, Lee a notch or two above six feet, but the way they talked about these little women made them seem pretty small. You got the idea that *the little women* were all bigger than the men.

For example, the big thing in Clark Lee's life, besides the little woman, that is, was something that he called the *chalk line*. He often drew this line, with his finger, across his desk. Or if he was stand-

151

ing he would draw this line on the air. The little woman expected him to walk that line, he said. Perhaps he did, as this line always seemed to be with him, either there on his desk, drawn on the thin air, or like a pattern in the rug. A line drawn between Clark Lee and everything else. "With the little woman," Lee would say, "I got to toe that line!" and he would tap on it, putting out his feet to where he saw something on the rug. It would be wrong to say that this line was imaginary. It was there in the lobby, in his office, in the sidewalk when he stepped in the street, and it hung like an invisible clothesline in the air. Ready to trip him or support him, as the case might be. Big man though he was, Clark Lee often seemed to lean on it.

Perhaps *the little woman* was sometimes on Will Brady's mind, those long summer evenings, when he stopped in at the Paxton to see if Evelyn Fry was there. She sold cigars, but she was no cigar-counter girl. She knew the one Will Brady had married—she was a married woman herself—and she always asked him how his *kids* were getting along. Sometimes Evelyn Fry like to go for a ride where they could just sit and look at the river; other times she would make him a cooling drink of something in her rooms. The fellow she had married had left her a lot of furniture. There were tasseled lamps, a grand piano with a shawl and some photographs, and sometimes there was a smell stronger than the incense she liked to burn. A cigar, but that was all right too. That was something they had both come to understand. These things didn't matter so much any more, and perhaps the thing they had in common was the knowledge of what things seemed to matter and what things did not. A cigar or two didn't. Which was why he was often there.

Sometimes he would sit there with the glass of beer she was sure he would like if he would just drink it—until the foam was gone, the beer was warm, and she would drink it herself. Other times he had grape juice with lumps of ice in it. He would suck on the ice while she played him records on the gramophone. Perhaps she thought he was homesick, lonely, or something like that. It probably meant she was sometimes lonely herself.

He liked to be with Evelyn Fry just to be with her, to sit there in the room, and to stir the ice in what he was drinking with one of her spoons. While the music played, nobody had to talk. He would sit facing the piano with the hanging shawl, the vase with the red paper flowers, and the picture of a gaunt-looking man in his underwear, rowing a boat. Her husband. He had left her, naturally. He had a stiff black beard and it had probably tickled her face.

"That song," she would say, putting on the record that he seemed to like, but never knew the name of, "what is it you like about it so much?" Did he ever answer? No, he never had to say. He had ice in his mouth, and perhaps he didn't know, anyhow.

That was how he liked to put in an evening—not too often, just now and then—when he had the need of a little woman for himself. Someone to pour him a drink, and ask him simple questions about his kids. And around ten o'clock he would leave, as he had to go and pick them up. If they were at the Empress, but not in the lobby, he would ask the manager, Mr. Youngblood, to run the slide advertising Will Brady's Chickens and Eggs. This would let them know that he was in the lobby waiting for them. But if they were at the World, or the Orpheum, where slides like that had gone out of fashion, he would just sit there in the lobby until they came out. People like Tom Mix, Hoot Gibson, and Wallace Reid they liked to see twice, which took a good deal of time if six acts of vaudeville came in between. In that case he would buy a bag of popcorn, and the usher would let him sit in the lobby as they had all got to know him and knew pretty well what his problem was.

But in August he found the boy in the lobby alone. As that usually meant that the girl was in the ladies' room for a moment, he sat down and waited while the boy finished eating a peanut bar. When the girl didn't come, he said: "Son, where is your mother?"

"She left," said the boy, "she left before the vaudeville."

"Your mother left?" he said.

"She went off with the Hawayan," said the boy. "He liked her and she's going to work for him."

"A Hawayan?" he repeated.

"She's going to dance for him," the boy said. "If I could dance I'd have gone to work for him, too."

IN THE LOBBY

1

In the suburbs Will Brady owned a fine house
with a chain swing on the porch, a playroom in
the basement, and a table in the kitchen where he
left pocket money for the boy. But both the boy
and the man did their living somewhere else. The
boy did all of his living next door—that is to say,
he added one more plate to the table that already
numbered three on each side and one at the end.
So it was the boy's plate that evened it up, as Mrs.
Ward said.

When Will Brady walked over to discuss the
matter, there was really nothing that remained to
be said, as the boy had been living—Mrs. Ward
said *living*—with them for some time. If he passed
the night at home it was merely to make his father
feel all right. Nobody liked to sleep in a big empty

house alone. All Will Brady could do, speaking up when he did, was recognize what had already happened and offer to pay, as he did, for the boy's board. It was agreed that he ate around five dollars' worth of food a week. He was small, but a small growing boy could somehow stow it away. It was also agreed that his father should continue to buy his clothes. These matters taken care of, Mrs. Ward agreed to let him see the boy, once or twice a week, and give him pocket money so long as it wasn't too much. She took away from him sums that she didn't think it wise for a boy to have. In case the boy got sick, or really needed something, or might, for some reason, just want to see his father, Mrs. Ward would leave a message for him at the Paxton Hotel. That was where Will Brady, for the time being, had taken a room.

When a man has lost something he would like to get back, say a wife, a boy, or an old set of habits, he can walk around the streets of the city looking for it. Or he can stand on a corner, nearly anywhere, and let it look for him. The boys and girls Will Brady found under the street lights, or playing around the posters in the theater lobbies, didn't know what he had lost but they had learned what he had to give. They could hear the coins that jingled in the pocket of his coat. If he stood on the corner, a well-lighted corner, sooner or later they would gather around him—just as the pigeons would gather around him when he sat in the park. They didn't know what he wanted, but they were willing to settle for what he had to give.

"Hello there, Harry," Will Brady would say, as he liked to call all of them Harry. As it was never their name, it gave them something to talk about.

"My name ain't Harry," they would reply, then: "Gimme three cents."

"What you going to do with three cents, Harry?"

"My name *isn't* Harry!" they would say; then, getting back: "if I had three cents I could go to a show."

"So you think you'd like to take in a show, Harry?" he would say.

"You gimme three cents an' I'll have ten."

They were smart, these kids, and so they would talk for quite a while. Sometimes it took quite a bit of handling—knowing when to stop calling them Harry—but with a pocket full of pennies a man like Will Brady could talk for an hour.

"Don't tell me, Harry," he would say, "I've got a grown-up boy of my own. I can tell you a thing or two about boys."

"What can you tell?" they would ask, and of course he couldn't tell them much of anything. Nothing but what he had read about this Tom

Sawyer, or this Penrod. They were the only boys, it seemed, that he knew very much about.

And as for girls, he knew even less—no, he didn't know a thing about girls until the one called Libby —Libby something—spoke to him. On 18th and Farnam, near the *Omaha Bee*, somebody ran out from the shadows toward him, and he assumed it was one of the boys, some skinny kid.

"Well, Harry," he had said, "is this a holdup?" and put his right hand into his pocket before he really knew—before he looked, that is—at the sharp freckled face. The girl was tall and thin, and the dress she had on was too small for her.

"Well, well," he repeated, "is this a holdup?"

"No, sir," she said, "it's not holdup," but he couldn't see her face as she stood between him and the light. He stepped to one side to look at his hand —in the palm of his hand were coins, most of them pennies—and she came around to lean over his arm, look at them too. She put her small head between him and the light. It was narrow, and the long black hair was in braids. The braids were hooked over her ears, like pulleys, and as she peered into his hand she tugged on them, slowly, tolling her head like a bell.

"That ain't enough," she said.

"For a show?" he said.

"For kisses," she said, "I'm sellin' kisses." When

he didn't speak right up, she said: "I'm not beggin' anything, I'm sellin'.""

"I see," he said, and raised his head as if someone had called his name. He looked to the corner where swarms of bugs flew in and out of the street light. Passing beneath the light were a man and woman, the man with his coat folded over his arm, and the woman a step or two away from him, as if he were hot.

"Twenty-five cents is what I try and get," she said, "but if that's all you got, it's all you got," and with her dirty brown fingers she removed the coins from his hand. One at a time, pecking at his palm like a bird. When she had them all she stepped forward, putting up her face, rising on her toes, and gave him a noisy peck on the cheek. Then she stepped back, moving out of the light, to see if he was pleased.

"That wasn't so much," she said, "but it was fourteen cents' worth. Wasn't it?"

He agreed. "Oh yes," he said, and wagged his head.

"But I can do better," she said, and lifted her arms as if she were a dancer, letting her hands, the fingers parted, droop at the wrist. From a bench in the park Will Brady had seen little girls drop their jacks, or the doll they were holding, and throw up their arms, their heads back, as if they would fly.

Without warning, as if some voice had whispered to them. Sometimes it was pretty, other times it was like what he saw now. She leered at him over her left shoulder, her eyelids fluttering, and he knew he had seen it all less than an hour before. On the Orpheum billboards, where two beautiful girls were wrapped in gauze. Maybe he looked unhappy, for she said: "Did I take all your money?"

"Oh no," he said.

"I'll bet I took your carfare," she said, and looked at the coins in her hands. The dime she removed, held out to him.

"No, no," he said, "and besides, I walk. I like to walk on nights like this."

"Me too," she said, and danced around him, swinging her braids. Still dancing, she said: "And I know what you're thinking."

"What?" he said.

"That I'm not old enough. You're thinking I'm not old enough to take care of myself." He shook his head. "Well, that's what you're thinkin', you men."

"You're quite a big girl," he said.

"I am. I make my own livin'. I make up to five dollars a week. Isn't that good?"

"That's a very good living."

"It's more than my father makes," she said.

164

Still facing the light, he said: "What does your father do?"

"Nothing," she said, and sang that a bridge was falling down. She danced around him twice, singing, then she stopped singing, hopped up and down, and ran toward the corner, where she suddenly stopped. Her dress was too small, and she drew it down toward her sharp knees. Then she turned to wave at him, her long braids swinging, and was gone.

2

Two, sometimes three or four times a week, she "did business with him." It was strictly a business proposition, as she said herself. The fact that he seldom had the right amount of money didn't trouble her much. Sometimes she would have newspapers under her arms, usually old papers, which she would sell him, as she was in business, she told him, for herself. But kisses were a better proposition, as they cost her nothing. All she had to do was find somebody who wanted them.

On the week ends, when she specialized in kisses, she wore a large flowered hat with a flapping brim, and in the crown of the hat there were many flowers, some of them real. But what he smelled, as she always had to tell him, was her perfume. It was sometimes so strong that as she rose toward him he closed his eyes.

Inside her dress, these nights, she wore a brassiere, the pink cups folded over very neatly, and in the one on the right she kept all the money she made. It jingled as she ran off or stood hopping up and down. Week nights she had to be home early, but Saturday nights she had time to talk, if that was what he wanted, or a marshmallow sundae, if he wanted something like that. As her shoes hurt her feet, they usually had the sundae sitting down. In the ice-cream parlor she would take off her hat, as the veil on the hat tickled her face, and sometimes fell in the marshmallow sundae when she closed her eyes. She always closed her eyes, as ice cream tasted better that way. He would have a cherry phosphate, or a root beer, and when her mouth was full, and her eyes were closed, he would sit there looking at her sticky, freckled face.

Was he in love with her? That was what she wanted to know.

He said he wasn't sure. He said he didn't know.

He ought to make up his mind, she said, because if he was in love with her, really in love, he could kiss her without paying anything.

In the Lobby

Was she in love with him?

She didn't know. No, she didn't know, she said, a whole lot about love. She didn't know if what she felt was what she had heard, or if what she heard was what she felt about it. She didn't know if she had ever loved anybody or not. When she had a baby she would probably love it. Then she would know. Then she would know if what she felt for him was love or not.

Eating and talking also made her sleepy, and she would let him walk her home—to the corner, that is, where she kissed him for nothing. He could see the rooming house where she lived, the cracked yellow blinds, the old men on the porch, and watch the gas jets flutter when she closed the door at the end of the hall. Then he would go home, lying awake in the hot front room across from the boy, watching the flash in the night when the street-car trolley was switched around. When the last car for the night went back into town.

During the day he had eggs in his hands, things that he could pick up, that is, and put down, and tell what they were, good or bad, by holding them to the candler. But during the night there was nothing he could grasp like that with his hands. You can't take a notion into your hand, like a Leghorn egg, and judge the grade of it. You can't hold it to the light, give it a twist, and see that it is good. Nor is there any way to tell if it is what you are missing or not.

Could a man say, for instance, that what he really needed was a woman's hat? A cheap straw hat with a wide flapping brim, a long pin through the faded paper flowers on the crown. A hat made of yellow straw, shiny with varnish, with dried marshmallow stuck to the veil, and both dark and blond hairs tangled in it. All of its long life it had been just a hat, an inexpensive straw hat no longer in fashion, and then one day, in spite of itself, it was on a new head. It became, overnight almost, something more than a hat. It became a notion—something missing, that is, from a man's life.

So that when this girl Libby took off this hat and set it on the marble-topped table beside her, the man seated across from her might put out his fingers and touch the wide brim. He might sniff at the flowers, or take between his fingers a torn piece of the veil. Just as he had once, standing idle on the corner, let his hand rest for a moment on a boy's knobby head, or let his fingers tangle for a moment in the wild hair. But when this boy got away some man would say—some stranger, that is, would step up and say—"If you want to handle the kids, you better get 'em off the street."

And what do you say to that? Why, you say thank you, thank you very much. Maybe this

168

stranger has what he calls your own interests at heart. Thinks that he is doing you a personal favor to speak like that. But a hat, after all, is just a hat, and if you want to lean over and sniff the paper flowers, or touch a piece of the veil, why that is perfectly all right. Very likely it was something you put up your own good money for.

But near the end of the summer he found the girl in a telephone booth at the back of the drugstore, and in the booth with her, sitting there hugging her, a fat blond boy. They had been to Krug's Park, and the boy's pink face was badly sunburned. On the lapel of his coat, like a lodge button, was a live chameleon. The boy said: "Howdy, Mr. Magee," as he naturally assumed Will Brady was the girl's father, but he stayed right there in the telephone booth, with one arm around the girl. She was giggling over the phone about boys to some other girl. Will Brady looked at his watch, put it away, advised them to have a nice time that evening, then walked out into the street before he noticed what he held clasped tight in one hand. A handful of coins: five pennies, two nickels, and one shiny new dime.

That was not the last he saw of the girl, but she no longer ran toward him out of the shadows, or wore on her birdlike head a wide flappy-brimmed hat. The braids were gone, and the dirt now showed behind her large ears. He would see her in the battered front seats at the Empress, sitting there with some boy, or some middle-aged man, the pale light of the screen blinking on her powder-dirty face. The large mouth open as if to help the eyes drink it all in. And later, like a sleepwalker, she would walk into the luminous glare of the lobby, where, with one finger, she would loosen the wad of gum from her front teeth. Facing, but not seeing him, she would start chewing on it.

3

WELL, that was how it was, and if it sometimes seemed strange, it was hardly any stranger than anything else, and not so strange as the fact that only in hotel lobbies was Will Brady at home. Somehow or other he felt out of place almost everywhere else. In the houses that he bought, or in the rooms that he rented, and even in the cities where he lived. But in the lobby of a good hotel he felt all right. He belonged, that is—there was something about it that appealed to him.

He liked to sit in a big armchair at the front—in

a leather-covered chair if they happened to have one, and under a leafy potted palm, in case they had that. He also liked a good view of the cigar counter, and the desk. He liked the sound of the keys when they dropped on the counter, the sound of the mail dropping into the slots, and the sound of the dice—though he never gambled—in the stiff leather cup. God knows why, but there was something he liked about it. Hearing that sound he immediately felt at home.

A curious artificial place, when you think of it, glowing nightlike by day, and daylike by night, with no connection whatsoever with the busy life that went by in the street. And when a man came in through the revolving doors, it was the man that changed. The dim, shaded lights and the thick carpeted floors cast a spell over him. His walk, what you think of as his bearing, the way his arms moved or hung slack from his shoulders, all of these things were not at all what they had been in the street. He took on the air of a man who was being fitted for a new suit. A little bigger, wider, taller, and better-looking than he really was. And on his face the look of a man who sees himself in a three-way glass. In the three-way mirror he sees the smile on his face, he sees himself, you might say, both coming and going—a man, that is, who was from some place and was going somewhere. Not the man you saw, just a moment before, out there in the street.

A man comes into the world, you might say, when he steps into his first lobby, and something of this knowledge brings him there when he expects to depart. If something is missing, the lobby is where he will look for it.

And yet no two lobbies are exactly alike, there is a difference in the rugs, or the lighting, in the women at the desk, the price of the cigars, and the number of plants. There will sometimes be a difference in the men and women you find in them. There may also be a difference in the marble columns, their thickness through the middle, the height of the ceilings, and the quality of brass—if that is what it is—in the cuspidors. There will often be a difference in the service, the age of the bellhops, the location of the men's room, and the size of the carpets at the sagging side of the beds. But the figure in the carpet will be the same. Not merely in the carpet, but worn into the floor. A man seated on the bed could feel it through his socks, recognize it with his feet. All hotels are alike in this matter, and all the lobbies are more alike than they are different, in that the purpose of every lobby is the same. To be both in, that is, and out of this world. The same things go along with lobbies that go along with dreams, great and small love affairs, and other arrangements that never seem quite real. The lobby draws a chalk line around this unreal world, so to speak. It tips you off, as the closing of the hymnbooks tips you off in church that the song is finished and that it's time to get set for the prayer. It prepares you for a short flight from one world to a better one. From the real world, where nothing much ever happens, to the unreal world where anything might happen—and sometimes does. But there is no mystery about it. It is just a matter of rules. Just as there are hard and fast rules in the street that make it impossible for some things to happen, so there are rules in the lobby that make it possible. You can sense that as you come through the door. You can breathe it in the scented air, hear it in the women's voices, the creak of leather luggage, and the coin dropped on the counter for a good cigar.

And the name that is written there in the ledger? Take a look at it. Is it Will Brady, or is it William Jennings Brady, or is it perhaps just Will Jennings, as it doesn't really matter, for the time being?—you can be whom you like. And as for that young woman there at your side—is that your wife? You hope so. That is the gist of it. For it is the purpose of hotel lobbies to take you out of the life you are living, to a better life, or a braver, more interesting one. More in line with your own real powers, so to speak. The porter cries aloud a name in the lobby and you turn, for it might be yours, and perhaps you have never met this stranger before, your better self. You can see him in the eyes of those who turn and look at you. To size you up, to compare you with their own better selves. Just as there are men who are never lovers until they meet their wives in the lobby, there are women who have never been loved anywhere but in a hotel room. Only there does the lover meet the beloved. In the rented room is where men exceed themselves. Lovers and seducers, prosperous, carefree men of the world. What you find in the lobby, what you hear in the music, what you feel in the air as you saunter across it, is the other man and the other woman in your life. There in the lobby the other life is possible.

Perhaps that man at the counter, rolling the dice, is the one who made the Beautyrest mattress possible—but not the sleep. No, you can't have everything. You can't manufacture the good night's sleep and sell it with the bed. But, still, it is something to know that the sleep would be a good one, and that the man responsible for it is quite a bit like yourself. Middle-aged, paunchy, and often subject to lying awake.

And when you've lost something you would like to get back, the lobby is where you can look for it, sit waiting for it, or, if you know what you want, you can advertise. As you probably know, it is smart to advertise. Adam Brady did it when he wanted a wife, Will Brady did it when he wanted an egg, as the only problem is in knowing what you want. Knowing, that is, how to put it in ten or twelve words. But that can be quite a stickler. Take something like this:

> FATHER AND SON seek matronly woman take charge modest home in suburbs.

Was that what he wanted? Well, he thought it was. But he would have to wait and see what an ad like that turned up. If what he said, so to speak, had covered the ground. On the advice of the girl in the office, he ran that ad in the "Personal" column, as he was looking for something rather special, as she said. He gave his address, of course, as the Paxton Hotel. The lobby would be just the place for a meeting like that. It would not be necessary for him to inquire what such a woman had in mind, as it was there in the ad, and all the woman had to do was answer it. That was what he thought, this fellow Brady, when he took his seat at the front of the lobby, wearing the look of a man who was the father of a homeless boy. That was what he was thinking when a Miss Miriam Ross asked to speak to him.

"Hello," she said to him as he came forward. "Where'll we park?"

With the hat that he held, Will Brady gestured toward the back.

"Okey-dokey," she said, and walked ahead of him with her shoulders back, her hips thrown forward, with the motion of a woman going down a flight of stairs or a steep ramp. From the back Will Brady could see the rolled tops of her stockings, the red jewel clasps, and when she sat down— dropped down—he saw them at the front. He had never seen a flapper before. Not up close, that is. He wondered if, over the years, he had fallen out of touch with the motherly type.

Miriam Ross lay in the lobby chair, her arms wide, her legs spread as if the room was too hot, and smoked cigarettes while peering at him dreamily as he talked. What did he say? Something about himself and a homeless boy. Every now and then he fanned the blue smoke away from his face. Now and then the girl sighed, as if tired, or tipped her head to blow the smoke in her lap, or make little cries, like a puppy, while dusting her cigarette. Later she leaned forward, on her sharp knees, to powder her face. On a piece of gum wrapper she wrote her name, her address, and her telephone number, then she slunk along before him, coughing softly, toward the door. "Be seeing you, daddy," she said, and patted him gently on the chest.

When you know what you want, perhaps you still have to learn how to ask for it.

> FATHER seeks large matronly
> woman to mother homeless boy.

Was that too .plain? He would drop the *large*. Somehow, when he was a boy, matronly women were all large.

> FATHER seeks matronly woman
> as companion growing boy.

Perhaps it was best to keep the father out of it. He let a week pass, then he ran this ad in both the Des Moines and the Omaha papers, and in the following week he received eighteen replies. He made appointments with a Miss Lily Schumann, a Miss Vivien Throop, a Bella Hess, and a Mrs. Callie Horst. Mrs. Horst's letter to him had been very brief:

> *I sometimes get so sick and tired of all of them.*
> *How old is yours?*

Mrs. Horst also lived on a farm and didn't know, whether she could get to town within the month or not. But his first appointment was with Miss

Schumann, who would be wearing, as she said, white feathers, a fur muff, and a red handbag. She also described herself as stylish stout.

He found Miss Schumann seated near the phone booths, asleep. She was well dressed, her hands in a fur muff, and her corset hugged her body so that it seemed to prop her upright, like a barrel. Now and then she burped, putting out a pink tongue to lick the film from her lips. She was rather short, with small hands and feet, and from time to time her brows arched up, her face flushed, and her small white teeth would bite down on her lip. She seemed to be digesting, and enjoying it very much. Without opening her eyes she removed from her handbag a small handkerchief, with blue tatting, and wiped her full lips, both inside and out, like a baby's mouth. Later she dropped a green mint on her tongue. Her small hand, with the fat fingers, rested on her muff like a picked bird, and when she sighed, her breath was scented with wintergreen. He let her sleep. She was still there in the lobby, blowing softly, when he met Miss Throop.

Miss Throop lowered herself—she did not sit down, nor drop down, she lowered herself—as her glasses, on a cord from her throat, swung back and forth beneath her large bust. "Throoooop," she was saying, "old English," and when she was lowered, her legs crossed at the ankles, she felt about on her front where her glasses had once been. This was on the top of her bust, rather than beneath. "Throoooop," she repeated, and found her glasses in her lap.

Miss Throop had spent the best years of her life as a tutor to the Countess Moroni, companion and tutor to her three lovely children and the Countess herself. This was of course in Italy. During the morning she and the children spoke only Italian and French, during the afternoon they spoke English and American. American was the hardest—she had been away so long. It bored her to death—were they seated in a draft? She stood up, wheeling, and backed herself against the radiator. Did he mind a woman standing, she asked, and spread her full skirts to catch the heat. She simply felt *better* standing—that was what years of lecturing did. As the heat billowed her skirts, she fluffed them out, let them fall, and the sweetish sour smell hung over the lobby, the smell of soiled clothes. She was getting warm, and the bangs of her wig, a crisp amber color, stuck to her forehead when she raised her hand, patted them down.

"And now tell me," she said, with her fingers on her eyelids, "about your son."

While Will Brady talked, Miss Throop inhaled
her own rich smell. She stood with one hand at her
back, the other raised to her damp forehead, with
the tip of the thumb and the first finger on her
lidded eyes. Her glasses had made deep blue bruises
at the bridge of her nose. Under her arms the colors
had run, the dress snaps had parted, and there in
the open were the shiny spears of her corset stays.
When he stopped talking, for a moment, she turned
to look at the rain.

"Rain, rain, rain, rain, rain, rain," she said, and
gave her skirts a toss, like a dancer; then as they
drooped she felt around once more on the top of
her bust. But it was not for her glasses. Smiling, she
said:

"You mind if I smoke?"

Bella Hess said no, no thank you, she'd just as
soon stand up and talk, and looked about her as if
the lobby chairs were so many beds, the pillows
rumpled and the covers thrown back. Bella Hess
had worked for years in Cedar Rapids, and she
handed him a letter, several pages long, describing
the cooking, the washing, and the hundred extra
things Bella Hess had done. She had along with her
a small bag of hard rolls, another letter of recom-
mendation, and a wicker case with an umbrella
strapped to the side. Will Brady just stood there,

holding the letter, until Bella Hess picked up her bag, took the letter from his hands, and walked through the swinging doors into the street.

The next woman he met did not even trouble to answer the ad. She just happened to be standing in the lobby when he was speaking to Bella Hess, and while he stood there, wondering, she came up and spoke to him. She had a powder-stained face, bleached hair; but there was something familiar about her—about the walk, and about the way she rolled her eyes. Like the weighted, rolling eyes of a sleeping doll.

"You lookin' for somebody, daddy?" she said, and stepped so close to him that she touched him, with her head tipped back as if there was something caught in her eye—something that he, with the corner of his hanky, would have to remove.

"I am interviewing housekeepers," he said. God knows why, but he said it, and saw that her teeth no longer looked cold in her red mouth.

"You're doin' what, daddy?" she said, and pressed so close to him that he could see the pores in her nose. They had always been large. Yes, he remembered that. "I'm not so good at keeping house, daddy," she said, "but there's other things I can tend to," and she took his coat by the lapels, drew him down toward her lips. He was unable to move, or to

181

speak, and when he saw her tongue wagging in her
mouth, like a piece of live bait, he closed his eyes
and put one hand to his face. At the front of the
lobby someone rattled the dice, and he saw, as if
cupped in his hand, the face of the girl behind the
cigar counter at the Wellington. She had rocked
the leather cup and said: "Come have a game on
me."

"You sick, daddy?" she said.

"No," he said, "no, I'm all right," and opened
his eyes and looked at this strange missing woman,
his wife.

IN THE CLOUDLAND

1

AFTER putting his wife to bed, Will Brady came downstairs and took a seat in the lobby, facing a railroad poster of a palm-fringed island in a soft blue sea. A glass-bottomed boat, with many bright flags flying, the deck crowded with happy men and women, sailed from a white pier—so it seemed to Will Brady—toward happiness. The island of waving palms seemed to float in the blue —the pale blue of the sky, the deep blue of the sea —and to be nothing more than what men were inclined to call a mirage. But the name of this place was Catalina, and it was said to be real. It could be found, like the town of Omaha, on a map somewhere. And according to the message on the poster, this island was just two days away—just two days and three nights from where he sat in the Paxton

Hotel. Out of this world, and yet said to be in it at the same time.

In Will Brady's mind what the girl needed, what this strange woman, his wife, needed, was what he had often heard described as a change. It was linked in his mind with white Palm Beach suits, the shoes that Lyman Bryce wanted him to wear, gay beach umbrellas, and a wide view of the sea. Off there, if anywhere, the grease and paint would wash from the girl's stained face, her dyed hair would grow dark, and in time he would recognize her. And in the meantime he would go through a change himself—hard to say in advance just what it would be —but they would both begin, as he had read in books, their life over again. So he let it be known that Will Brady and his wife would be away several weeks. That seemed to be the time that it took to effect a real change. Then he stepped up and ordered, from the clerk at the desk, two round-trip tickets to California, with a passage to that island advertised on the poster—if there was such a place.

But two long days and three nights on a train can seem quite a while. He hadn't seen this girl, his wife, for some time, but after one good meal in the diner it seemed that he had run out of things to talk about. There was a good deal to see out the wide diner windows, and a good deal to eat, sitting

there, but when you run out of talk the long days
seem to drag. Fast as they were traveling, even the
view was slow to change.

Was it twelve or fourteen telephone poles to the
mile? Watching the poles file past like wickets, he
thought of that. The red and white road markers
were faded now, and the bleak frame houses, like
bumps on the land, looked as lonely and forgotten
as an abandoned caboose. It reminded him of something. He had traveled west with this woman before. At that time the painted bands on the poles
were new, the winter wheat in the shimmering
fields was new, and the girl and the boy, there in
the seat beside him, were new as well. In a certain
way, he must have been fairly new himself. A
second-hand label might have looked strange on any
of them. But now that new coat of paint was gone,
the white band on the poles had faded, and he didn't
have to look at himself to know other things had
faded as well. Nor did he have to be told that the
town down the tracks would be Calloway, a whistle
stop now. He saw the fine City Hall was like a
birthday cake without the frosting, and a strip of
tattered flag was flapping from the stilts on the
water tank. The word DOMINOES had been painted
on the window of the Merchant's Hotel. Down the
spur of weedy track he saw the lumber mill, with
a few weathered boards in the yard, and beyond it

the frame house with the clapboards peeling, the
windows smashed. He remembered there had been
a creaking flight of stairs on the east side. Now
they were gone, the lantern was gone, but the rust-
colored scar, like a gash, was there, with the tattered, blowing strips of a Hagenbeck & Wallace
circus poster. The mouth of the rhinoceros, like a
great hole in the wall, was still there.

The good will prevail, Anna Mason had said, but
sometimes a man was led to wonder. Was it possible that a man died just to be dead? The answer
was no—if you had to answer a question like that.
Will Brady's father had died, his mother had died,
and around five thousand leghorn chickens had
died, but certainly not for nothing. No, they died
to give him a piece of advice. What was it? Well,
it seemed to have faded a bit as well. Something or
other about how, in the long run, the good would
prevail.

Hadn't he, for example, found his wife? After a
change and a rest wouldn't she be as good as new?
If he sometimes lay awake at night just to look at
her face while she was sleeping, it was merely because she looked more like her old self that way.
During the day he found it better not to look at
her. He didn't know the face. The woman he saw
looked like somebody else.

For a while it did him good to see her eat—the

rest and the food would do her good, he thought—
but watching her eat, his own appetite began to
fall off. He stopped eating. He settled for a cup of
coffee now and then. As this meant there was food
left on his plate, she would reach for the toast he
didn't eat at breakfast, dip it into his egg, and then
finish off his marmalade. She poured his cream into
her own coffee, asked for more of it. In the last
swallow or two of her coffee she liked to dip the
lump sugar, suck out the coffee, then leave a heavy
syrup in the cup and on her lips. Between meals she
ordered sandwiches from the porter, and if the
train stopped at a station she would lean out the
window to buy candy bars and fruit. She couldn't
seem to eat enough, sleep enough, or even see
enough out the wide windows, as if every moment
that passed might be her last. In the evening he read
to her from some movie magazine.

In the window that he faced he could see her
tongue coming and going as she washed her teeth,
explored her gums, or found bits of food in her
mouth that she had stored away. There were little
pads of fat, like sideburns, in her puffy cheeks.
Stage make-up had coarsened her skin and there
was a deep-blue stain, like a bruise, that would not
wash out from beneath her eyes. It was part of her
face, like the distracted baby-roll of her eyes. She
used the white tongue to pick her teeth, and every

now and then, facing the window, she would stick it out and have a look at it.

At night she slept with her mouth open, which was normal enough in some ways, except for the change that it brought to her face. Her body, all of this time, remained the same. There seemed to be no connection between this body and the face. This may have been why she could eat all day long and half the night, feeding her face, without her body showing any signs of it. The face had gone off, was going off, that is, somewhere on its own. But the body was faithful—put it like that. The body was faithful even though the face seemed to find the world too complicated, the going too rough, and the living too sick at heart.

From the Biltmore Hotel, in Los Angeles, in the big red cars chartered for that purpose, they rode down to the sea where there were piers, crowds of people, and amusement parks. Facing the sea there were benches, and seated in the sun, wearing the dark glasses, Will Brady would read from the guide-book to her. He kept himself posted in order to point out the interesting things. From a glass-bottomed boat they peered into the sea at schools of fish, drifting like birds, and in the evening they would sit on a terrace somewhere, watching young people dance. Now, however, no young man came

forward and spoke to her. It seemed to be clear
that the woman at his side was not his child. Out on
the dark sea were the lights of boats, pleasure craft
as some people called them, and across the water,
sparkling like stars, were the lights of the shore.
Very much as if the sky—or the world they were
now in—was upside down. Which was not at all
strange as that was how this world really was.

There were people who told him that the City
of Angels was an unreal city, a glittering mirage,
and that the people were as strange, as rootless, and
as false as the city itself. That the whole thing was
a show, another mammoth production soon to be
featured in the movie houses, and that one fine day,
like the movie itself, it would disappear. Will Brady
couldn't tell you whether that talk was true or not.
But he could tell you that part of the description
was real enough. This unreal city, this mammoth
production full of strange, wacky people like himself, was an accurate description of a place Will
Brady recognized. Here, bigger than life, was Para-
dise on the American Plan. A hotel lobby, that is,
as big as the great out-of-doors.

Every morning they rode off to look at something described in the guidebook or pictured on
the cards, or they sat in the lobby, where other
people came to look at them. Or they rode out in
buses to watch the great lover, John Gilbert, make

191

love. They saw him kneel, one knee on the floor, and make love to the woman whose eyes looked bruised and whose armpits were sore where she had just been shaved. In the sun a small boy walked an aging lion about the streets. Over a cardboard sea great towers fell, and men leaped from the windows of burning buildings to fall into nets held aloft on wooden spears. Half-naked women, in skirts of straw, lay about on a floor sprinkled with sand, their bodies wet from the heat of great smoking lamps. Thick custard pies, suspended on wires, made their way around corners, and curved around poles to catch the man—the villain, that is—full in the face. Beyond, the mountains rose up to be seen from the valley, and the valley dropped down to be seen from the mountains, and so that nothing might remain unseen the dry air was clear. And one went to bed, in this unreal world, but not to sleep. The eyes were closed, it seemed, the better to look at onself.

All that Will Brady saw he kept to himself, perhaps lacking the words for it, but what the girl saw when her eyes were closed kept her awake. Lying there in the dark, as she had years before, she would talk. Once it had been men that troubled her sleep, but now it was herself. During the day he sometimes wondered if she saw anything very clearly, but during the night she seemed to have eyes like a cat. She saw everything. Even stranger, she had the words for it.

There was a Mr. Pulaski—or so she said—who took her for long buggy rides in the country, where he would fish, with a pole, while she played at rowing the boat. In the afternoon he took naps, lying with the newspaper over his face, and she ate chocolates and shooed the flies off his big hands. They were red on the back, with knobby knuckles, and the nails of one hand were blue from how he had worked in Poland, the old country. He napped with his hands lying at his side, like a dead man. He was good with horses, and they would run without his whipping them. Every week he gave her a five-dollar bill, saying: "Now you go and buy yourself something," but that wasn't what she wanted to do. He kept giving her money for something she didn't want to sell. He was very nice, but she stopped seeing him.

There was a Hazel Roebuck, who was head cashier at the Moon. Hazel Roebuck knew in advance when Wallace Reid or Francis X. Bushman was coming, and she would give her tickets for the mezzanine seats free. Hazel Roebuck had a nice room at the Paxton Hotel and she liked to have help while trying her clothes on, taking a bath, or doing any number of things. There wasn't anything that she liked to do alone. She liked to let down her long hair and let someone do it up, or leave it long and try on broad-brimmed summer hats. She showed her what ice would do to the nipples of her breasts. Hazel Roebuck did not give her money, but she left her with the feeling that what she got, she got for nothing, so to speak. As she didn't want it for nothing, she stopped seeing her.

There was a Mr. Marshall, who was head floor-walker for Burgess & Nash. He wore expensive clothes like an actor, a paper flower on his coat, and, under his vest, buttons that held his shirt pulled down. As he was the last man out of the building, they could use the ladies' lounge, or the men's dressing-room on the second floor. He would sit on a chair and patiently watch her take off her clothes. He liked her to undress so that all of her clothes fell in a puddle at her feet, except her black stockings, which he liked her to leave on. Then he would give her all new clothes to put back on. He never once put his hand on her, said anything nasty, or giggled, and everything that she could wear out of the store she could have. In the winter that was quite a bit. He was very shy, and the first man ever to call her Miss Long. He didn't give her money, or tickets, but when she had all of the clothes she could wear, summer and winter, she had stopped seeing him.

Did she *like* him? he had asked. He had interrupted her to ask her that.

Like him? she had said. Oh, she had liked him all right.

Did she feel any *love* for him—that was what he meant to say.

No, she had replied, she hadn't felt anything like that. It was Francis X. Bushman who had awakened her to love.

When she recognized it for what it was she sat in the movies eight hours every day, loving him and hating the women that he kissed. That was love. A woman only felt like that just once.

What about—he said—what about himself?

Whatever it was, she said, it was not love at first sight. Maybe it was not what she would call love at all. She might not have even looked at him if it hadn't been for the way he looked, and the way he didn't seem to know what to do with himself. He just sat there in the lobby. Or he got up and went for long walks. All the other men she had ever known were able to talk, to smoke, or do something, but he just sat there without doing anything. He had money, wavy brown hair, and strong white teeth like Mr. Pulaski, but the first time she saw him she simply didn't feel anything. The second time maybe she felt sorry for him. Then one day, God knows why, she saw what was wrong. She saw that Will Brady knew how to give, like Mr. Marshall and Mr. Pulaski, but what he didn't know was how to receive anything. Maybe what she felt was love the day that she saw that. Maybe she really loved him, that is, the day that she saw that he was hopeless—or maybe what she felt was something else.

Getting back—he said—getting back to other men besides himself, just what was it that she felt for them?

For *them?* she said.

The other men in her life. What did she feel for the other men in her life?

Sorry, she said, she felt sorry for them.

Just what did she mean by that, he said, what did she mean by feeling sorry?

They were moths, she said, that flew away from the flame.

And where, he had asked her, where in the world had she picked up *that?*

It was a line in one of her plays, she said. In this play she would climb out of the bed, or if she was out she would climb in it, and the man in the bed or the room would run away. She would call to him that he was a moth afraid of the flame. Everybody would laugh. Why did they laugh?

It was the way of men to laugh, he said. That was their way.

Was he different, then, she said, from other men?

Was he? Did she mean that he had been burned? Did she mean that he, Will Brady, had not run away from the flame? Did she mean that all the other men had got out of the bed or hid beneath it, or did she mean that all the other men were part of the play? She liked this play? he asked.

She liked the view from the stage.

The *what?* he said.

She liked the view. From the stage she had a good view of all of them.

Them—? he said.

The men, she said. It was like a new show for her every night. They came to see her, they paid their good money, but the light from the stage was on their faces and she didn't have to pay a cent to see all of them. And they didn't care—they all wanted her to look at them. So she made it a point, lying there in the bed, to look at each man in every row, and if the town was big and the house was full this took time. It might take her two or three weeks to see all of them. If the show had a long run, as it often did in the larger places, sooner or later she saw most of the men in town. Five or ten thousand men, some of them single, some of them married with wives and children, some of them rich, some of them poor, some of them good and some of them bad, but every living one of them there to be seen, and to look at her. She knew them all, and all of them knew her. But they were all moths, she said, that flew away from the flame.

It made him smile, lying there, to hear her talking in terms like that, and to think that of all these men she had picked him out to be burned. When she had held the flame up to him, he hadn't run. Some people would say that he hadn't even sense enough to do that.

But he didn't laugh, as he might have, or ask her if she thought he was such a fool as to believe the only men in her life had been under her bed. No, he didn't ask her. He didn't even bring it up. The longer he lived the easier he could believe wild talk like that. He didn't find it hard to believe at night, and it didn't strike him as silly in the morning when he took a seat, with the other old men, on a bench in the park. In the unreal world, talk like that seemed real enough.

On the one hand you would say that the old men in the park had either lost or given up something, like the ratty-tailed pigeons that paced up and down on the walk. They had given up the notion of being some fancier kind of bird. They were no longer ashamed to let their feathers drag on the walk. On the one hand you could see they had given it up, on the other hand there was a man

called Teapot. That was the only name that he had
—where had he picked it up? Every morning, like
the sun itself, he entered the park. To the casual
passer-by it might appear that this fellow Teapot
had some kind of trouble, bodily trouble, that
forced him to walk along with one hand on his
hip, the other raised in the air. But those who knew
better knew that this fellow Teapot had become a
new thing. No longer merely a man, he was a Teapot. He was meant to be poured.

"Brother, pour me!" Teapot would say, and the
brother would take Teapot by the arm, as you
would kettle, and tip him forward till he poured.
Whatever Teapot contained would flow out the
long spout of his arm. "Thank you, brother," he
would say, and proceed across the square. Later in
the day, several times, he would need to be poured
again. Now, there were people who would class
Teapot as odd, or even downright wacky, but Will
Brady had acquired a different feeling about such
men. Put it this way: he felt right at home with
them.

Every day Will Brady saw, on the bench near
the fountain, an old man with brown bare feet, his
soiled pants legs rolled, and three or four wiry hairs,
like watch springs, on his flat, leathery chest. He
passed most of the day with a newspaper spread
over his face. Morning and evening he fed the

pigeons, wetting the hard dry bread in his mouth, rolling it into a ball, then feeding this spittle to the birds. Some of the old men in the park sat and wagged their heads over something like that. But not Will Brady. No, he felt very much at home.

Was there any man, Will Brady asked himself, who didn't understand something like that? Who wouldn't like, that is, to be fed to the birds himself? Well, there were several men who said the old fool with the bare feet had a brain that was soft. Sitting in the sun, they said, had done that to him. The old man's hands, lying in his lap, had got to be the color of walnut stain, and if he napped sitting up, the pigeons roosted on his shoulders, dirtied his front. It soon dried in the sun and he chipped it off later, absently. The way Will Brady would chip the hen spots off a Leghorn egg. In one pocket of his coat the old man kept reading matter, in another pocket eating matter, and every hour or so he got himself up and took a long drink. He would peer through the palm trees at the clock to see how much time he had passed.

Was this an example of what the sun would do to a man? Perhaps it was, as Will Brady passed the time that way himself. The great problem in life, as any old fool could tell you, was not so much about love, or the man and the flame, nor did it have much to do, in the long run, as to who it was that was burned. No, the real problem was nothing more than how to pass the time. Every day it was there, somehow it had to be passed. The really great problem in life was merely how to get out of the bed in the morning and put in the time until you went to bed again. The girl solved this problem by lying awake at night, having breakfast in bed, and trying to sleep during the day. Will Brady got up and sat on a bench in the park.

In the early evening the girl would get up and they would go out some place for dinner, but one evening, after his walk, she was not there. Neither in the lobby nor up in the room. That usually meant she would be in the ladies' room, and he took a seat near by in the lobby, across from a tall flat girl who stood in the door chewing gum. This girl seemed to take an interest in him. On the seat beside him was a magazine open at a picture of Pola Negri, but Will Brady couldn't keep his mind on what he read. The girl in the door kept staring and smacking the gum. So he put the magazine back on the seat, took time to look at his watch, but when he walked across the lobby the girl followed him. Before he could make a getaway she said: "You lookin' for somebody, daddy?"

"I am waiting for my wife," he replied.

"Adds up to the same thing," she said, and when

he looked at her face she smacked the gum she was chewing, sucked in on it. "You got a nice long wait," she said, and when he didn't answer that, she added: "I'd just as soon sit down, daddy," and then she pushed through the swinging door and walked into the street. He followed her. She was wearing the kind of clothes that the girl liked to wear. A shabby fox fur hung from her shoulders, and the shriveled grinning head, with its glassy eyes, bounced on her hip. He walked behind her to the corner, where she turned and said: "This be all right, daddy?" and nodded her head toward the corner drugstore. As they went in she called to the waitress: "Make it a double chock-Coke, honey," and as they sat down at the back she took her gum from her mouth, stuck it to the seat.

"You have seen my wife?" Will Brady said.

"Not any too good," she said, "she was on the floor, and it was hard to see her." He stared at her, and she said: "Daddy, you want me to begin at the first?"

"Why, yes," he said, and felt his head nodding. When the girl brought the Coke he asked her for a cup of coffee, black.

"First you get a bottle, daddy," she said, "then you lock yourself up in a nice pay toilet, then you empty the bottle, and then after while you fall off the seat. When you fall off the seat I come along and pick you up."

"Thank you," he said, "very much."

"Oh, I'm paid for it," she said, and tapped a cigarette on her thumbnail. "I'm paid," she said, "but God knows I've done it ,for nothin' enough." She lit the cigarette and blew the smoke in his face.

"She's all right, then?"

"Daddy," she said, and closed her eyes. With her eyes closed she let the smoke drift through her nose. "Daddy," she went on, "a nice man like you makes a bad girl like me feel better. You owe it to a girl—where'd she pick you up?"

"Miss—" Will Brady began.

"Clinton," she said, "Flora Clinton."

"Miss Clinton," he said, "if you have seen my wife—"

"You a Mr. Metaxas?"

"Brady," he said, "Will Brady."

"Next time you pick up a little girl," she said, "say you look in her handbag and see who she is. Say you find out whether you're a Mr. Metaxas or not." He looked at her, and she said: "Well, daddy, you asked for it."

He turned from Flora Clinton and looked at the Palms in Pershing Square. The old man with bare feet was feeding the pigeons from a paper bag. He wet the food in his mouth, then spit it out nd fed it to them. The flapping of their wings stirred the stringy hair at the back of his head.

"You mind a personal question?"

"No," he said, and wagged his head slowly.

"Where'd she ever find you?"

"Omaha."

"Where is that?"

"It's a town on the Missouri," he said, and saying that, he saw it there before him, a town on the bluffs. He saw the muddy river and the new toll bridge they had put over it.

"That must be a great place," she said, "Omaha, I'll remember that," and took from her purse a small card, wrote a number on it. She handed it to him and said: "Next time you feel like a little girl, daddy—"

"This woman is my wife," he said.

"That makes it even worse, daddy," she said, and finished her Coke. There was ice in the glass, and she tipped her head back till it spilled into her mouth. Then she patted his arm and said: "I've got to run along now, daddy," and stood up from the table, smoothed the wrinkled front of her dress. "You say this kid was your wife?" she said.

"This woman is my wife," Will Brady replied.

"I don't get it," Flora Clinton said, "I don't see why she didn't talk." She looked at her face in the mirror, then said: "When people don't talk they think they're in love. Maybe she was so drunk she thought that she was." That made her smile, sucking in the air from the side of her mouth, where a tooth was missing. "Well, bye now, daddy," she said, and he watched her walk away.

From the corner, where he stood at the curb, Will Brady watched the old fool who was feeding the pigeons, and saw on his face the rapt gaze of a holy man. A circling flock of pigeons hovered above him, flapping their wings. On the old man's face was the look that Will Brady had seen, many years before, on one of the calendars at the foot of his mother's bed. A religious man, it was said, who fed himself to the birds. So it was not a new notion. No, it was a notion of the oldest kind. Very likely this old fool let himself think that in just such a manner he might fly himself, grow wings like an angel, and escape from the city and the world. As the spirit is said to escape from the body, when the body dies. Perhaps he thought that—or perhaps all he was doing was making love. There were many ways to make it, after all, and perhaps that was one of them.

No voice had ever spoken to Will Brady before —or even whispered to him, for that matter—but now from out of the sky, above the noise of the pigeons, one spoke to him.

"Old man," this voice said, "so you think you are a lover?"

Did Will Brady smile? No, he kept a sober face.

"Speaking of heaven," the voice went on, though of course they had not been speaking of heaven, "I suppose you know there are no lovers in heaven. I suppose you know that?"

"No lovers in heaven?" Will Brady replied, but the voice did not answer. Will Brady thought he heard it sigh, but it might have been the wind. "Then why go to heaven?" Will Brady said.

"I don't know," said the voice, "I've often wondered." Then it added: "But I suppose the small lovers like it. They like it up here."

"And the great lovers?" Will Brady said.

"There's no need," said the voice, "for great lovers in heaven. Pity is the great lover, and the great lovers are all on earth."

That was all, that was all that was said, but somehow Will Brady was left with the feeling that this creature in heaven, somehow, envied every old fool on earth. That something was missing in heaven, oddly enough. As it had never occurred to Will Brady that something might be missing in heaven, he turned to watch the pigeons wheeling over the park. They were rising, and filled the sky with the sound of their wings. On Will Brady's face, strangely enough, was the rapt, happy gaze of a holy man, like the old fool who stood barefooted in the park. Together they watched the pigeons wheeling until they were gone, the sky was void, and the old man suddenly threw into the air his flabby brown arms. Over his head, for a moment, floated the empty paper bag.

IN THE WASTELAND

1

H E HAD asked the porter to wake him out of Cheyenne. That was not necessary, however, as he was wide awake, his eyes were open, when the porter rattled the curtains of his berth. With his pajama sleeve he wiped a small hole in the frosted glass. A new fall of snow, like a frozen sea, covered the earth. In the spring and the fall, through the wide diner windows, a man who had felt hemmed in by the city, or who had had, as he thought, enough of people, might find relief in the vast emptiness of the plains. He might feel what some men felt when they came on the sea. In the winter, however, there was no haze to soften the sky, blur the far horizon, or lead a man to think that he might, out there, make a go of it. Everything visible had the air of being left there, dropped

perhaps. Every mound or post had the look of
cattle frozen upright. Will Brady, for example, had
seen such things as a boy. It was strange to find
them, after so many years, still vivid in his mind.

He could see the winter dawn, a clear ice color,
and far out on the desolate plain, like the roof of
the world, were two or three swinging lights. He
could make out the dry bed of the river, and as the
train was stopping for water, he could hear, down
the tracks, the beat of the crossing-bell. The rapid
throbbing of this bell, at such a godforsaken and
empty corner, seemed to emphasize that this scene,
the birthplace of Will Brady, was as remote, and
as dead, as a crater on the moon.

As the train slowly braked to a stop, he could
see the frame of the cattle loader, and then, suddenly, the station along the tracks. A lamp, with a
green glass shade, hung inside. It threw an arc of
light on the wide desk, the pads of yellow paper,
and the hand of the man who sat there, a visor
shading his face. The fingers of this hand were
poised over the telegraph key. His head was bare,
getting bald, and the green celluloid of the visor
cast a shadow the color of illness on his face. He
was staring, absently, into the windows of the
passing cars. On the table before him lay a bamboo
rod, curved at one end like a plant flowering, and a
sheet of folded paper was inserted at the curved

end. Will Brady saw all of this as if it were a picture on a calendar. Nothing moved, every detail was
clear. He could smell the odor of stale tobacco, and
the man's coat, wet with snow, gave off the stench
of a wet gunny sack. He could see the wood stove,
just back from the light, and he thought he could
hear, out there in the silence, the iron ring of the
ground where a brakeman stamped his feet. In the
man's dark vest were several red-capped pencils,
and as Will Brady gazed at his face he raised his
head, suddenly, as if a voice had spoken to him. He
gazed into the darkness where Will Brady lay on
the berth. And Will Brady fell back, he held his
breath, and as his hands gripped the side of the
berth he heard again the mechanical throbbing of
the crossing-bell. He seemed to see, out there on
the horizon, the snout-like mound of the buried
soddy, where he had been, even then, the last man
in the world.

He closed his eyes, and when the morning
light came though the window he drew the blind
to keep it from his face. He did not rise on his elbow to look at Murdock, or Calloway. Nor did he
get off at Omaha, although that was his destination,
and the conductor came back through the car to
speak to him. Where was he going? Well, he
hadn't made up his mind. He was going where the
train was going, and when that turned out to be

213

Chicago, he implied that that was all right with him. All the roads seemed to lead to Chicago, so there was no reason why Will Brady, who followed the roads, shouldn't go where they led.

2

To GET to Menomonee Street in Chicago you take a Clark Street car in the Loop and ride north, twenty minutes or so, to Lincoln Park. If you want to get the feel of the city, or if you like to see where it is you're going, you can stand at the front of the car with the motorman. On certain days you might find Will Brady standing there. Not that he cared where he was going, but he liked the look of the street, the clang of the bell, and the smell of the track sand that came up through the floor. He liked to stand with his hands grasping the rail at the motorman's back. At certain intersections he liked to turn and look—when the door at the front opened—down the streets to the east where the world seemed to end. It didn't, of course, but perhaps he liked to think that it might. When it did, as one day it would, he wanted to be there. On up the street he could see the park, and in the winter, when the trees were bare, he could make out the giant brooding figure of Abraham Lincoln himself. Soft green, like the color of cheap Christmas jewelry, or the fine copper gutters on the homes of the rich.

Lincoln Park was right there where the street angled. He could see the Moody Bible Tabernacle, and at the next stop Will Brady would step forward and get off. Menomonee was the street that went off like an alley to the west. To get to 218 on this street he would follow the curb on the north side to where this number was nailed on the first door on his right. The second door was the entrance to Plinski's delicatessen store. The first door was usually kept shut, even in the summer, to make the rats from the store go around and use the stairs at the rear. But the second door was open until ten or later every night. There was a sign on the door saying as much, but anyone who lived in the room overhead, and who tried to sleep there, didn't need to be told.

Will Brady lived in the room at the front, over the screen door that slammed with a bang, in a room that was said to be suitable for Light Housekeeping. To get to this room he walked up the stairs, along the bright-green runner of roach powder, and at the top of the stairs he took the door on his left. It opened on a small room with two windows on Menomonee Street. The window on the left was cut off by the bed, but over the years and through many tenants one window on the street had proved to be more than enough. On a winter afternoon it might even be warm, as the slanting winter sun got at it, and by leaning far out one could look down the street and see the park. An ore boat might be honking, or the sounds of the ice breaking up on the lake.

Inside the room was a small gas plate on a marble-topped washstand, a cracked china bowl, a table, two chairs, a chest of drawers, an armless rocker, an imitation fireplace, and an iron frame bed. Over the fireplace was a mirror showing the head of the bed and the yellow folding doors. The bed was in the shape of a shallow pan with a pouring spout at one side, and beneath this spout, as if poured there, a frazzled hole in the rug.

To get from the stove to the sink it was better to drop the leaf on the table and then lean forward over the back of the rocking-chair. On the shelf over the sink were four plates, three cups and one saucer, a glass sugarbowl, two metal forks, and one bone-handled spoon. On the mantelpiece was a shaving mug with the word SWEETHEART in silver, blue, chipped red, and gold. In the mug were three buttons, a roller-skate key, a needle with a burned point for opening pimples, an Omaha street-car token, and a medal for buying Buster Brown shoes.

In the Wasteland

At the back of the room were the folding doors that would not quite close.

To get to the bathroom, the old man who lived in this room would open these doors, greet Mrs. Plinski, then proceed to the back of the house. Mrs. Plinski was usually there in a rocker, nursing her twins. In the bathroom, seated on the stool, was her oldest boy, Manny Plinski, watching his baby turtles swim around in the tub. Manny Plinski was seventeen years old and had the long narrow face of a goat, big wet eyes, and a crown of silky, corn-yellow hair. This hair grew forward over his face and he stroked it forward, with a raking motion, as if there was something tangled in it that would not comb out. When he was displeased, Manny Plinski would make a sound like priming a pump. Mrs. Plinski would put down the twin she was nursing and wet her fingers under the tap, then sprinkle Manny Plinski as if she was dampening clothes. That would make him all right, and he would just sit there, staring at his turtles, or he could be led out in case you wanted the bathroom to yourself.

That wasn't very often, as the old man had got to be fond of the turtles, nor did he seem to mind Manny Plinski just sitting there. He would wink at the boy while the lather was thick on his face. Manny Plinski never laughed, but if he was pleased he would take one of the turtles, one that he liked, and slip it into the pocket of the old man's pants. The old man, somehow, never seemed to catch on to this. Later, of course, he would find it there and cry out for help. For a man so fond of turtles it was strange how they nearly scared him to death.

Leaving the bathroom, he would come back through the house, nod to Mrs. Plinski, then pass through the folding doors without closing them. He would let them stand open, as if his room was part of the house. He could see out, or any Plinski that cared to could see in. If a turtle was missing, this would be Manny Plinski, raking his hair in an excited manner; otherwise it might be Mrs. Plinski herself. What did she want? Well, the old man in the room had spoken to her. He had called out, perhaps, to ask if she had ever heard the likes of this. A clipping of some kind, or a passage from a letter spread out in his lap. So she would get herself up, this woman, in spite of the twin she was nursing, and brace herself, as she often seemed tired, between the folding doors. One heavy arm she would prop on the door, as if it weighed on her. The old man himself, seated at the table, would have the long sleeves of his underwear rolled, as otherwise they dragged in the food on his plate. He would be eating; that is, he had been eating, but he had stopped eating in order to examine, as the writing was fading, the letter in his lap. Two sheets of yellow paper, each sheet with widely spaced green stripes. The top sheet spotted with grease like a popcorn bag. The old man had spread the letter in his lap as his own fingers might be greasy, or in order to open, with the bent prong of a fork, the plugged hole in a milk can.

The letter was not new, it was cracked at the folds, and there were coffee stains in the margins, but it described in considerable detail an unusual event. How a snake, taken sick at the stomach, threw up a live frog. It described how the boy, the writer of the letter, picked this snake up by the tail, twirled him like a rope, and then watched him whoop up this poor frog. Not many city people would be familiar with anything like that. Mrs. Sigismund Plinski, for example, who had lived for forty-six years in Chicago, had heard the letter many times but couldn't seem to get enough of it. She would just stand there, wagging her head, as she did when the world was too much for her, and listen to the old man read parts of it aloud. Sometimes he just read the last of it, which he thought was particularly clever, and then went on to read how the boy had signed his name.

Your son—Willy Brady Jr.

that was what it said.

"You would think," the old man would say, put-

219

ting the milk can down on the table, "that a boy who could write a letter like that would write a little oftener." Not that he meant it, of course, as a smart boy like that had things on his mind. It was enough for him to know that his father was sometimes one of them.

"Oh, how he must love you!" Mrs. Plinski would say. "Oh, how he must love you!" and that would be all. In some respects that was about all that she ever said. Then she would wag her big head, with the loose flesh on it, and roll the little eyes that were too small for her face. "Oh, how he must love you!" she would go on, and before Will Brady went on with the letter, or read the passage over, he would blow on the coffee that was already cold in his cup. It was never hot, but it seemed to do him good to blow on it.

"Mrs. Plinski," he would say, "now you know how boys are," and indeed Mrs. Plinski did. Both men and boys. If she knew anything, that is, this woman knew that.

"How he must love you!" she would repeat, and shift her great weight as her feet were tired, and whichever twin it was, astride her haunch like a saddle, would be asleep.

Once a year this boy wrote to his father, and maybe ten or fifteen times a year Will Brady wrote, but somehow never mailed, a postcard to his son. It would have a picture of the park or the wide blue lake on it. But every month Will Brady expected to move into larger, more homelike quarters, and when he moved—the very day that he moved—he would mail that card. It was there in his pocket, already stamped and addressed. All he had to do was put his own new address on it. This address would be—as he told everybody—over facing the park. There would be trees and grass when the boy walked to the window and looked out. There would always be a cool summer breeze blowing off the blue lake. Every year he had to write this card many times as the writing would get smudgy from the dirt in his pocket, or even the picture on the front of the card would begin to fade. So he would buy a new one, in the hotel lobby, and seated at the table where the pens were chained, he would write on the back in such a manner that it also showed on the front. It had got so the message was more or less the same. It was always spring on this card, the same robin always caught the same worm.

Dear Son—

Have moved. Have nice little place of our own now, two-plate gas. Warm sun in windows every morning, nice view of park. Plan to get new Console radio soon now, let you pick it out. Plan to pick up car so we can drive out in country, get out in air. Turning over in my mind plan to send you to Harvard, send you to Yale. Saw robin in park this morning. Saw him catch worm.

Sometimes he said radio, sometimes he said coupe, every now and then he put Princeton instead of Yale, but he always held out for a place of their own, a nice view of the park. He always insisted that the robin caught the worm. Perhaps that was why, after three years, he was still in the room over the delicatessen, and why that postcard with the view of the park had not been mailed.

It might be wrong to say that Will Brady, an old man in yellow underwear with the sleeves rolled, lived in this room any more than he lived anywhere else. He slept there, or tried to sleep there, and that was enough. It gave him certain habits that he found very hard to break. All during the day the screen door slammed, strange children ran in and out of the hallway, and the old man who sold snails seemed to sell most of them right in one spot. Will Brady would lie there, listening to the strange cry that he made. He could hear the snails scooped out of the tub, hear the man put his hand in the striped popcorn bags, and then hear the shells when the little boys stepped on them with their heels. A powdered sound, like the track sand, but without the fresh flinty smell.

The room in which he lay had folding doors that would not quite close. The boy named Manny Plinski often stood there peering in. He was said to be a mute, that is to say that he couldn't speak in the usual manner, nor understand very much, nor do very well at the other boys' games. But the old man in the bed seemed to understand him pretty well. They had found there was very little that needed talking about. Once a week, in the good weather, the old man and the yellow-haired boy might be seen in the zoo, facing one of the cages of monkeys, bears, or strange exotic birds that looked and sounded like Manny Plinski himself. If there was a difference it was not in the feathers, nor in the cage. The man who came to feed them never stopped to sprinkle water on them.

In Will Brady's room was an iron bed, several chairs, and what a man might need to do a little housekeeping, but these things were not, strictly speaking, inhabitants. Like Brady himself, they might easily be taken away. One morning Mrs. Plinski might peer in and find them gone. But while the room was there, there would always be the smell. It was there in the floor, in the plastered walls, in the draft that stirred but never departed, in the idle curtains, and in whatever clothes hung on the back of the door. Day in and day out, winter and summer, this smell was there. A stranger might refer to this smell as a stink, as some of the lodgers were loose in their habits, and another might notice the odor of the grease, and the stale coffee grounds. But only Will Brady knew this smell for what it was. It was the smell of man. And there was something that he liked about it.

This smell was in the lining of the brown coat that both the sun and sweat had faded, and everything in the pockets, old or new, had picked up the scent. The money in the wallet, and the letter even before it was read. Once opened, and read, the letter might be said to be full of it. The message might fade, but with every reading the smell increased.

"Just listen to this," Will Brady would say to Bessie Muller, the waitress at the Athens, and read her that part about the boy and the frog-sick snake. She was a farm girl herself, but she had never seen a snake carry on like that. Or get sick at his tummy just like she did.

"You would think he liked his father," Will Brady would say, "to sit down and write him a long letter like that," and Bessie Muller would agree to that, naturally. She would even point out that nobody—*no*body—was writing letters to her.

"That kid sure likes his daddy," she would say,

and take one of the bobby pins from her hair, clean her nails with it, and then bend the point between her chipped front teeth.

If the night was warm Will Brady would walk past the moss-green statue of Abraham Lincoln, then on across the tennis courts with their sagging nets and the blurred chalk lines. There would be men with their shoes off padding around in the grass. There might be women with white arms in the shadows, fussing with their hair. Under the sheets of newspaper, with what was left of the food, some child would lie asleep.

If there was a moon, or a cool breeze off the lake, Will Brady would walk through the park to the water, where he would stroll along the pilings, or under the trees on the cinder bridle path. He had walked on cinders, he seemed to remember, somewhere before. As he had in the past, he would have to sit down and tap them out of his shoes. In the dusk there would be lights on the Wrigley tower, an airplane beacon would sweep the sky, and at Oak Street beach people would be lying in the warm sand. The drinking fountain would give off a strong chlorine smell. He would wet his face at the fountain, then take his seat among those people who had come to the beach but didn't care to take off their clothes; who had been hot in their rooms, and perhaps lonely in their minds. In the dark they could speak what they had on their minds without troubling about their faces, the sound of their voices, or who their neighbor was. Will Brady was their neighbor. He sat with his coat folded in his lap, his shirtsleeves rolled.

All over the wide beach he could see the white legs of the men, the white arms of the women, and the half-empty milk bottles propped up in the sand. Matches would flare, cigarettes would glow like fireflies. He could hear someone wading, and see the water foam at their feet. When the excursion boat left the North Pier there would be a lull in the beach murmur, and men would rise on their elbows, as if awakened, to watch it go by. They would crane their necks as if they feared to miss something. The red and green boat lights would swing on the water, the music blow in, then out again, and later the long white wave would draw a line on the beach. And after the wave, if there was a breeze, the music again.

"I see by the paper," Will Brady would say, and smooth the sleeve of the coat he was holding, "that it was over a hundred in western Kansas to-day."

To whom was he talking? Perhaps the murmuring air. It had come, one might say, from Kansas itself. Many things had. Perhaps the old man seated there on his left.

"Bygod, now that's hot!" this old man says, and rubs the balls of his eyes with his knuckles, as if he could see—could look back to Kansas and see for himself. He stares at the night, cranes his head, then makes a blowing noise and says: "Kansas— what part of Kansas you from?"

"I'm from Nebraska," Will Brady says, "I'm a Nebraska boy myself"—though God only knows why he calls himself a boy. An old man more or less at the end of his run. "Born and bred in Ne- braska," he says, as if talk like that would revive him. "Got a boy out there now. He writes me that it's pretty hot."

"You don't say," the old man replies, and wets his lips. It would probably turn out that he had a boy somewhere himself. Or if he didn't, that he was small-town boy himself. Nearly everybody was. Where else was there to be coming from? It might surprise you how many men are small-town boys at heart, and how many small towns it takes to make a big one. Make it go, that is.

"The city's no place for a boy," Will Brady says, and gets to his feet as if that would end it. As if he didn't want to hear what the place for a boy was. "No, the city's no place for a boy," he would say, and then he would turn, look at the clock on the tower, and see that it was time for one old man to get back to work.

Another day he might not walk in the park at all, or even stop in at the Athens to see Bessie Muller, but he would go down Clark Street to the Gold Coast Café. He would sit at the counter and order one of their chicken-fried steaks.

"And how is your boy?" Mildred Weigall would say as she poured him a glass of water; she took it for granted that he would always order a chicken-fried steak. "Is he feeling his oats yet?" she would say, as she liked to think that he probably was, for she was young and feeling her oats herself.

"He's the outdoor type," Will Brady would reply, though it was hard to say what he meant by that. Did he mean that outdoor types didn't feel their oats? Probably not. Hard to say what he meant. It just so happened that one day Will Brady had sat there, reading a letter, when a snapshot of the boy had dropped out of the letter onto his plate. Mildred Weigall had wanted to know, naturally, who in the world it was. "Just a snap of the boy," Will Brady had said, and showed her that snapshot of the boy, without a stitch on, holding up one end of a canoe. But he was turned from the camera, so it didn't matter very much.

"Why, he's a nice-lookin' kid," Mildred Weigall had said. "Why don't you bring him around?"

"You think I'd try an' raise a boy like that back here?" Will Brady had said, and waved his hand, with the letter he was holding, toward the street. It had been snowing that day, and the street was full of slush.

"Not on your tintype," he had said; "kid's out in the country where he belongs."

"He's a nice-lookin' kid," Mildred Weigall had said, "he's got nice legs."

"Got his father's brains," Will Brady had replied, "and his mother's looks." That was pretty good. Somehow, it was always good for a laugh. "Thought I might bring him back," he had said, "just to show him what this place is like. But he wouldn't like it. He likes nature. Just take a look at this—" Then he would head her that piece about the frog and the snake. Like Mrs. Plinski, Mildred Weigall couldn't seem to get enough of it.

"He's a nice-lookin' kid," she had said. "when he comes, you bring him around."

On the left side of Clark Street, near Division, he passed a small movie house. Sometimes, just in idling by, he would see through the lobby doors, through the darkness behind, to the glowing silver screen. As if there was a crack in his world and he

could see into another one. For a moment he might
see, as if in a dream, men leaping from trains, trains
leaping from bridges, lovers embracing, or the flash
of guns in a battle scene. Or he might hear a song
—hear it, that is, from the lover's lips. One night
he had stopped, turning like a man who had been
softly tapped on the shoulder, to hear the love song
that came through the crack in the lobby door. A
love song, and a pagan lover was singing it. This
was something new, and, an old lover himself, he
surrendered to it. He became a young man more or
less without clothes, his strong tanned legs washed
by South Sea water, and with the sunset behind him
he sang this love song to his mate. *"Come with me,"*
the pagan lover would sing, and Will Brady would,
he came gladly, transporting himself to the land
of White Shadows, to the land of true love. There
he stood ankle-deep in the warm green water, sometimes spearing fish, sometimes singing love songs,
and sometimes, on the palm-fringed islands, making
pagan love. What kind of love was it? The doors
usually closed before he found out. He might have
bought a ticket, but perhaps he didn't want to
know. It was enough for him to know that the
young lover was there, still doing what he could.

Sometimes, standing there in the street, Will
Brady felt that perhaps he had died, but the man
in charge of him, the man this side of heaven, had

not closed his eyes. So he stood there, a dead man in most ways, but with his eyes looking out. Eyes that seemed to look backwards and forwards at the same time. An old sorter of waybills and a pagan lover at the same time.

Was he—or was that just a way of putting things? Perhaps he was in his mind, the one place that was more or less his own. For instance, just a block or so up the street was a library, with a desk near the door, and a friendly gray-haired woman sat there in charge of things. He had walked up to this woman and said: "What I have in mind is something on education, something on leading colleges, institutes of learning—"

"You have something in mind?" she replied.

"I have a boy," he said.

"Well now," she said, "that makes it interesting."

"The place to raise a boy," he had said, to show her he had thought quite a little about it, "is in the West, but the place to educate him is in the East." Now, that was sharp. He had read that in a book that she had given him. "Boy is also quite a writer for his age," he told her; "think he might become a writer of books himself."

"In that case," she had said, "he will need the very best this country affords," and that statement had come to mean a good deal to him. He had never really thought about it before, in just that way.

"That's just what I figure," he had said. "Right now I'm thinking of Harvard, thinking of Yale. Boy has a mind of his own, but I guess his father can think of these things."

"Yes, indeedy," this woman had said, which was a favorite expression of hers, and a sign that maybe she ought to get back to work.

He went without dessert at the Gold Coast Café in order to stop for a bite at Thompson's, where the coffee was good and there was a wider range of pie. The chimes would ring when he pulled his check from the checking machine. Mrs. Beach, the cashier, would smile at him, and if she was not too busy counting change, she would swing her chair around so they could talk while he had a bite to eat.

"And how is *our* boy?" Mrs. Beach would say, as she was a mother with four boys of her own, so there was nothing you needed to tell her about boys. When a picture of the boy had stuck to one of his bills—he carried it in the wallet along with his money—Mrs. Beach had insisted on knowing who this fine-looking boy was. Luckily, it was not the picture of the boy without his clothes. It was just his head, showing his mother's wavy black hair.

"Boy takes after his mother," Will Brady would say, and to that Mrs. Beach always answered:

232

"She must have been a very lovely girl—she certainly was that."

"Out of this world," Will Brady would say, and turn to blow on his hot cup of coffee. He would sip it, then add: "Died no sooner than the boy was born."

"You don't mean to say," Mrs. Beach would reply, "that that boy of yours has never had a mother?"

"Just me and the kid," Will Brady would say, and blow on his cup.

"Why, I just think you've done wonders, Mr. Brady," and it was clear that Mrs. Beach did. She couldn't imagine a boy without a mother like herself. "I just wish," she would sometimes say, "that she could come back for just an hour, just be with us for an hour, to see what a wonderful father you have been to him."

When she got around to that, Will Brady would turn to his pie. It was hard for him to straighten out the many things he thought. Rather than get into all of that, which might require quite an explanation, he would go back to the counter for another cup of coffee, drink it standing up. There were things that a mother like Mrs. Beach might find it hard to understand.

* * *

From Thompson's he went on down to Chicago, and some nights, there at the end of the street, he found the drawbridge rising on the sky, like a wall. The guard bell would be clanging, and the red lights blinking at the top of the span. In the bridge tower room, on warm summer nights, the man in the tower might lean out the window, the visor shadow on his face, and his shirtsleeves rolled on his thin white arms. He liked to spit in the street, and use a tenpenny nail to tamp down his pipe.

If the span was up, Will Brady would stop in LaMonica's Lunch. At that time in the evening Mrs. LaMonica would be cleaning up. On a sultry summer night she might be out in front, sitting there on a chair with her little girl Sophie, or in the back of the store cooking up tomorrow's hamburgers. She left the front door open as the back of the store would get pretty hot.

When he asked for coffee, Mr. LaMonica would say: "What the hell'd we do without a hot cup of Java?" and Will Brady, for the life of him, never seemed to knew. It seemed a simple question, but he never had an answer to it. Into his own cup of Java he would pour some of the cream from the milk can on the counter, a small can with two holes punched in the top, and the picture of a cow on the side. But Mrs. LaMonica, who had never seen a cow, liked her coffee black.

"When you know what I know," Mrs. LaMonica would say, rolling her eyes to think about it, "when you know what I know, you drink your coffee black." No doubt she knew a good deal, but it was never clear what she had against cows. She had never seen one. Perhaps that was it. But she had often lain awake at night and heard the moos they made going by in the trucks, and she smelled the empty trucks the next morning, on their way back. It was enough, anyhow, to make her drink her coffee black.

"Maybe a new prideswinna?" Mrs. LaMonica would say, and all because Will Brady, having nothing else to do, happened to mention that the boy had won a prize.

"Oh, nothing much," Will Brady had said, and showed Mrs. LaMonica the picture of the boy that had appeared in the *Omaha Bee*. The name was clear, but his face didn't come out very well. "*Tech student writes prizewinning letter*," it read. "You would think," he said to Mrs. LaMonica, "that a boy who can write prizewinning letters would find the time to write a few more of them to his dad."

"They're all of them no goddam good," Mr.

LaMonica said. He stopped frying hamburgers to say: "You start out all alone, and that's how you end up. You live long enough and bygod you're right back where you start up from."

"They're a comfort at the breast," Mrs. La-Monica said.

"A lotta good that does a man," Mr. LaMonica said, and slapped himself on the chest. "A hell of a lotta good!"

"A prideswinna is a comfort!" she had said, and there was no use in arguing the matter. Mr. La-Monica had tried. It was better to fry hamburgers.

"Well, I better get to work," Will Brady would say, "Or I'll never get him to college."

"Oh, Mike!" Mrs. LaMonica would say. "Col-litch—you hear?"

"If you and I were college men," Will Brady would say, when Mr. LaMonica turned to admire him, "we wouldn't be here. No sir, we'd be over on the Gold Coast."

"Now bygod you're right," Mr. LaMonica would say, and look to the east, where it was said to be.

Will Brady would take a toothpick from the bowl and say: "If the kid's going to do better than his dad, he's going to need the best this country affords. He's going to need the finest education money can buy."

"You hear that, Mike?" Mrs. LaMonica would say, but before Mike would answer Will Brady would get up, drop his nickel on the counter, and walk out into the street. Talk like that always made him excited, and he would be out on the bridge, over the water, looking down at scum, wide and green as a meadow, before he knew where he was. But the sight of all of that, and the smell of it, would cool him down. Something about that smell was like a good whiff of salts, the way it cleared his mind. But like the salts, it left him a little wobbly, walking along with his head in the air, and he usually tripped as he crossed the tracks in the cinder-covered yard. It would remind him to put away the letter, or the snapshot, that he still held in his hand.

3

IF THE old man who sorted waybills in the freight yards felt himself more alive there than anywhere else, it had something to do with the tower room where he worked. On one side of the room was a large bay window that faced the east. A man standing at this window—like the man on the canal who let the drawbridge up and down—felt himself in charge of the flow of traffic, of the city itself. All that he saw seemed to be in his province, under his control. He stood above the sprawling freight yards, the sluggish canal, the three or four bridges that sometimes crossed it, and he could look beyond all of these things, beyond the city itself, toward the lake. He couldn't see this lake, of course, but he knew that it was there. And when the window stood open he thought he could detect the smell of it.

Between Will Brady and this lake were thousands of people, what one might call a city in itself; people lived there, that is, without the need of living anywhere else. They were born there, and sooner or later they died. Mrs. LaMonica had lived there for forty-eight years, hating all cows and loving pagan lovers, nor had she ever found it necessary to go anywhere else. It was only necessary to have the money and to pay the price.

The bay window in the tower room was a frame around this picture. It hung there on the wall. The man in the room could stand there, at his leisure, and examine it. He would come to know, after a time, just what bulbs were out in which electric signs, and how the shadow of the bridge, like a cloud, moved up and down the street. If he was more alive there than anywhere else—if he seemed to come to life when he faced this picture—it had something to do with the fact that he was cut off from it. Which was a very strange thing, since what the tower room made him feel was part of it.

During the long day there were trains in the yard, and a great coming and going over the bridges; whistles were blown, and the tower room trembled when a train went past. But at night this old man, Will Brady, was alone in it. When the drawbridge went up he was on an island, cut off from the shore. Without carrying things too far it might be said that this tower was the old man's castle, that the canal was his moat, and that at night he defended it against the world. That is to say, that he felt himself the last man in the world. He was back—sometimes he felt that he was back— where he had started from.

In the windows along the canal the blinds were usually drawn, and behind the blinds, when the lights came on, he could see the people in the rooms moving around. Nearly all of them ate at the back of the house, then moved to the front. There they would talk, or sit and play cards, or wander about from room to room until it was time, as the saying goes, to go to bed. Then the front lights would go off, other lights come on. A woman would stand facing the mirror, and a man, scratching himself, would sit on the edge of a sagging bed, holding one shoe. Peering into it as if his foot was still there. Or letting it fall so that it was heard in the room below.

In all of this there was nothing unusual—every night it happened everywhere—except that the people in these rooms were not alone. The old man in the tower, the waybills in his hand, was there with them. He had his meals with them in the back, wandered with all of them to the front, listened to the talk, and then saw by his watch what time it was. With them all he made his way through the house to bed. He sat there on the edge, looking at his feet or the hole in the rug.

It seemed to Will Brady that he knew these people, that he had lived in these rooms behind the windows, and that he could walk about in the dark as if the house was his own. The life and habits of the house were not strange to him. No stranger, you might say, than that house down the tracks in Calloway, where a man named Schultz was said to have lived with a city girl. To have lost her, that was the gist of it. Quite a bit like what another old man, Will Brady, had done himself. As so many men seem to do—to have won, that is, and lost something—and to end up sitting at the edge of a bed, holding one shoe. Or to lie awake until the shoe upstairs has dropped.

From the tower room Will Brady could see all these people at their work, what they called their play, and the hours that they spent at what they called their sleep. Lying sprawled on wrinkled sheets on hot summer nights. Thinking. What else was it that charged the night air? That gave it that hum, that flinty smell like the sand crushed under the car wheels, until he felt that the lid to the city was about to blow off. And that the city itself, with a puff of sound, would disappear.

And then there were times—there were times toward morning when the city itself was as real as a picture, but the people who had lived in the city all seemed to be gone. Every man, woman, and child had disappeared. The lights still burned, the curtains still moved in the draft at the bedroom windows, and here and there, like a young cock crowing, an alarm went off. But there was something or other missing from the damp night air. The smell of man—as Will Brady could tell you—was gone from it.

What had happened? It seemed that the inhabitants had up and fled during the night. As if a new Pied Piper, or some such wonder, had passed in the street. Hearing this sound, they had rolled out of bed, or raised on one elbow as if the siren, the voice of the city, had leaned in the window and spoken to them. Beckoned, whispered to them, that the time had come. Nor were they surprised, as every man knew that it would. So they had risen, soundlessly, and gone into the streets.

Still there on the floor were their socks and shoes,

on the bedpost their ties, on the chair their pants, and on the dresser, still ticking, the watches they could do without. Time—that kind of time—they could now do without. They had marched off in the manner of sleepwalkers—and perhaps they were. They had moved in a procession, with the strong helping the weak, the old the younger, and what they saw—or thought they saw—out on the water, cast a spell over them. Perhaps it had been the bright lights on a steamer, or the white flash of a sail. But whatever it was, whether true or false, whether in their mind's eye or far out on the water, they had followed this Piper, followed him into the water, and disappeared. They had waded through the cool morning sand still littered with cigarettes, pop bottles, and rubbish, and without hesitation, like sea creatures, they disappeared. Nor was there any sound, none but the water lapping their feet.

So it was with those who had the faith; but there were others, even thousands of them, who wanted to leave, but they wanted to take the world along. They had brought along with them everything they would leave behind: magazines and newspapers, chewing gum and tobacco, radios and phonographs, small tins of aspirin, laxative chocolate, and rubber exercisers to strengthen the grip. Decks of playing cards, and devices to promote birth control. They had brought these things along, but the water would not put up with them. As they entered, it washed them back upon the sand. There it all lay, body and booty, like the wreckage of the world they had been departing, as if a great flood had washed it down to the sea ahead of them. In the pale morning light their bodies looked blue, as if they had been long dead, though living, and a child walked among them spreading sheets of newspaper over each face. As if that much, but no more, could be done for them. How live in this world? They simply hadn't figured it out. Nor how to leave it and go to live in another one.

Sunday morning Will Brady would walk through these streets, marveling at the empty houses, and gaze at the lake where the faithful had disappeared. He was not one of them, but it was a thing he could understand. He had his own way for departing one world, entering another one.

On these Sunday mornings he wore his Florsheim shoes, his Stetson hat with the sewn brim, and both the pants and coat to his Hart Schaffner & Marx suit. He did not walk in the sand, but in the grass at the edge of the bridle path. The Stetson hat, level on his head, he would tip to the ladies on the well-bred horses, their long tails braided, and a sudsy white lather between their hams. The ladies in turn would tip their heads, or lift their leather riding crops in a friendly gesture, as any man out for a walk, at that time in the morning, was one of themselves. One who preferred to walk rather than ride, but who was up like them to breathe the morning air before three million other people were breathing it. A thing reserved, by and large, for successful men. Men who hadn't the time, during the busy week, to idle and play like normal people, but who could make the time early Sunday morning, while normal people slept. Most of these men liked to ride, but there were others, like Will Brady, who were known to walk.

Both these men and women came down from the north, in the big cars with the very small seats, or they lived in the apartments overlooking the lake, along the Gold Coast. In these windows the blinds were always drawn against the morning sun. Uniformed men stood at the doors to these apartments, as they did before the fancy theater lobbies, but a man with Florsheim shoes, and the pants to go with them, could walk past. A man who knew when to à-la-carte, when to table-d'hôte. Such a man could walk into these lobbies, seat himself in a chair, examine the potted plants, or step to the desk and ask to speak to Mr. So-and-so. Will Brady usually inquired if a certain Will Jennings Brady was there. A big egg man from Texas, friendly, rather elderly.

So he would take a comfy seat in the lobby while the bellhop, or the secretary, or the manager himself would see that this matter was looked into. When he wore his Stetson hat, his soft leather gloves, and the hair combed back from his high forehead, quite a fuss might be made as to who this Will Jennings Brady might be. He would be paged in the lobby, and his name would stop the music in the dining-room. Words would be exchanged between himself and the management. Important gray-haired men, with their young wives, or perhaps it was their lovely flaxen-haired daughters, would pass in front of him with their thoroughbred dogs on a leash. Some of these dogs would stop and sniff at Will Brady's feet. They knew, these dogs, but they said nothing. Between the old man and the dogs there was quite an understanding, and they both needed it.

Sometimes Will Brady's fine voice would be heard in the lobby, also his laugh, perhaps a little strained, and that habit he had, when laughing, of cuffing himself on the knee, as if nailing that leg to the floor. Quite a performance, when you consider who this old man was. An old fool with one suit of underwear to his name. Just one pair of pants that he could cross at the knee like that. Naturally, Will Jennings Brady was never on hand, but one day an Ivy Brady, from South Carolina, spoke to him over the house phone and asked him to come right up. Hell, a Brady is a Brady, Ivy Brady said. But Will Brady asked to be excused as he had, he said, an important engagement with a big out-of-town man in the Loop.

But all of this took time—the sitting and the waiting, the patting of other people's dogs in strange lobbies, and the reading of papers left on the bench along the walk. The morning traffic would flow toward the city from the north, white sails would appear on the lake, and in the park life would begin all over again. Candy and peanuts were sold, men would roll the sleeves on white arms, put away for the winter, and women would sit fanning the flies away from baskets of food. Games would be played, young men would run and fall, others would stand in a row behind chicken-wire fences, and others would run toward Will Brady himself, waving him away. Crying that he should look up, or down, asking if he had eyes in his head. So he would make his way north, careful to avoid the deceptive clearing, where the unseen might be falling, or the games of young men who would suddenly turn and chase him away. The papers he found here and there he carried under his arm. It gave him the feeling that along with other people there was something in the park for him to do; also, he could sit on them in some places, in others he could read. It seemed to be the thing to do while waiting for the zoo to open up.

Later he would find himself a seat facing the strange big birds, or the melancholy bears, with an elderly man, about his own age, seated on his right. Not on his left, as that side of his face didn't feel right. There was an opening there that talking wouldn't fill up. He would take this seat, sighing, then say: "Kid writes me that there's bear where he is in the woods. Hardly a day, I guess, he doesn't stumble on a bear of some kind."

"You don't say!" That was what this man at his side would say. If he didn't, Will Brady would get up, sighing again, and try another bench. Sooner or later he would find a man who knew what was what.

"Only thing that worries me," Will Brady would go on, "is how a kid like that, a boy who loves nature, is going to like it in some place like Harvard or Yale. How he's going to like it in some quiet place like that."

It might surprise you how many men knew all about Harvard and Yale. Had a definite opinion, one way or another, on a subject like that. Had a boy there themselves, or a friend, or the son of a friend, or a brother, or some member of the family who had passed through there, going somewhere else. Who had seen it anyhow and knew what it was like. Nine out of ten men, you might say, seemed to have given either Harvard or Yale, or both of them together, more thought than Will Brady managed to. Their opinions, anyhow, were stronger than his own. They were either all for Harvard, without a quibble, or all for Yale. None of these men had been to college themselves—being tied up at the time with something or other—but they seemed to have a clear idea what they were talking about. They were glad to advise a man who hadn't quite made up his mind. Who had a boy who wasn't tangled up, as yet, with some damn girl. The general consensus seemed to be, in so far as Will Brady could order the matter, that great scholars went to Harvard and great athletes went to Yale. Albie Booth, for instance, he was going to Yale right now. But what about a boy who was showing signs of being both of them, an athlete and a great letter-writer at the same time? The first in his class, if it hadn't been for five or six girls. The place for a boy like that, one man told him in a confidential manner, was neither Harvard nor was it a place like Yale. It was Princeton, a place he had seen himself. He was a big man, with a beard, reduced to selling flags on pins for a living, but who nevertheless spoke with authority. As a boy he had passed— and he remembered it well—within a few miles of the place.

But it all took time—the life of the mind seemed to take as much time as a real one—and it would be midafternoon and the air would be hot when he started for the house. He would carry his coat folded over his arm and walk in the grass. His collar would be open and the Stetson hat pushed back on his head. Wherever tennis was being played he would sometimes stop and watch it, as the boy was said to be a coming tennis man. It helped him to see with his own eyes what the boy was. If one of the white balls came his way he would stop it, pounce on it, then hurry to where he could toss it to the players underhand. He had never learned to throw anything the other way. Tossing the ball, he would say: "I've got a boy who plays for Harvard," and then he might stand, if they would let him, close to the net. Some of them played very well, but it was clear that they were no match for the boy.

Sunday afternoons snails were sold on Menomonee Street. They were sold by a man who drove a small wagon, wearing on his own head nothing at all, but with three, sometimes four straw hats on the head of his horse. This was to make, as he said himself, the children laugh. He was a sad man and never laughed himself. He kept the snails in large tubs of water, and when he counted them into the bags, they made a sound like lead coins dropped on a slab. It was hard to tell the good snails from the bad. Most of them were bought by Nino Scarlatti, a boy with wild eyes and a curling harelip, and by Manny Plinski, who stood there with his money in his mouth. He would keep it there until he held the snails in his own hand.

After eating the snails, Manny Plinski liked to put the empty shells back in the bag, twist it at the top, and then make a fool out of somebody. That was always Will Brady, who would buy it for five cents. He would make himself a fool at the foot of the stairs, where the whole world could see him, and Manny Plinski would cry like a bird for his mother to come and look. So Mrs. Plinski would come, leaning over the railing, and Will Brady would stand there, a smile on his face, and with the nickel Manny Plinski would buy himself another bag of snails. "Oh, how he will love you!" Mrs. Plinski would say, and wag her big head.

On a hot summer day a big woman like that would not have much on. She would be in her bathrobe, or maybe her slip, with a damp towel thrown around her big shoulders, and she might have to stand there with her bosom gathered in her arms. In the winter she would be in the bone corset that made her arms stand out, as if she was crowing, and made it hard for her to scratch her back, pick her teeth, or get a comb into her hair. And in the corset she would always stand up rather than risk sitting down. She would stand between the folding doors, as if propped there, with her arms half raised.

"A new letter?" she would say. "A new winner?" And the old man there in the room, with his elbows on the table, would hold up the sheet of paper that he held in one hand. New? Well, hardly—the pages were torn at the folds. The light came through where bacon grease had been dropped on it.

"I was just wondering," the old man would go on, "what a boy like that"—he would wave the letter—"what a boy like that is going to do in a place like Harvard, or Yale?"

"Oh, how he will love you!" she would say, which it was hard, offhand, to picture the boy doing. But Mrs. Plinski was like that. A big, friendly woman who knew how it was.

4

I N T H E papers that he found in the park on Sunday mornings, Will Brady always read the want ads, as a man who wasn't quite sure what it was he wanted might find it there. Perhaps somebody, some man or woman, was looking for him. Perhaps a man like Insull had a position for him to fill. Perhaps—anyhow, Will Brady read the ads. And one Sunday morning—a cool November morning—he came on something that made him chuckle, made him put down the paper, rub his eyes with his knuckles, and wag his head. He looked around for someone to share it with, but he was alone on the bench. "Well, well," he said aloud, as he did with Mrs. Plinski; then he read it again.

MAN wanted for Santa Claus.

Now, that made him smile—he could feel the tightness at the corners of his mouth. It was enough to make him wonder, an ad like that—but he tore it out. He slipped it in with the letter and the photographs he had from the boy. Having it there in his pocket, as well as on his mind, he naturally showed it to Mrs. Plinski, asking her if she knew where they might dig up a good Santa Claus. Where Montgomery Ward—for that was who it was—could lay their hands on a man like that: a man big enough, fat enough, and of course out of this world. And then, just by way of a joke, asking her what she thought of a man like himself—a man like himself, that is, as Santa Claus. But this woman would surprise you. This woman didn't think it was a joke at all.

"How they will love you!" was all she said, as she seemed to have the idea that something like that was all you needed for a Santa Claus. It didn't seem to cross her mind that his cheeks, for one thing, weren't rosy enough.

As he had that ad right there in his pocket, he also showed it to Bessie Muller, asking her if she thought he was jolly enough for a Santa Claus. As a joke, of course, but she didn't take it that way.

"Why, you'd make a honey of a Santa Claus, pop." That was what she said.

"I don't know as I'm plump enough," he said.

"Oh, they put a pillow in you," said Bessie Muller, "you'd be all right. You'd make a honey of a Santa Claus."

Mildred Weigall thought the same thing. He didn't even show her the ad, he just happened to say that the one thing he missed, around Christmas time, was the right kind of Santa Claus. One that was, so to speak, really fond of the kids. Mildred Weigall had interrupted to say that she had known of kids, friends of hers, who had been pinched while they were sitting on the lap of Santa Claus. By the old bastard himself. That was what she said.

"If you don't like kids—" Will Brady had begun.

"You'd make a good Santa Claus," she had said.

"What they need is a man like yourself for Santa Claus."

Mrs. Beach said, holding the want ad close to her face, as she was nearsighted: "Why, Mr. Brady, all you need is just a touch of color on your cheeks." Then she looked at him as if she was the person to put it there. When Mr. Beach was alive, she went on, there was not a single Christmas that passed, in those happy days, that Mr. Beach himself wasn't Santa Claus. A big man—perhaps a little too big—he was especially good with other people's children, his own, of course, knowing him just too well.

He had been turning it over, Will Brady said, just turning it over in his mind, that he might at least stop by and look into it. He was alone pretty much, and it would give him something to do. It would at least be better than being alone at Christmas time.

"I think you'll find," Mrs. Beach said, "that they don't pay much."

"I just thought I'd ask," Will Brady said, and then put some toothpicks in his vest before going on to say that the pay wasn't what he had in mind. He had a job. The pay wasn't so important to him. "I just thought I'd inquire," he said, as, if the honest truth were known, it hadn't crossed his mind that a man would be paid for something like that. Was it possible they paid a man to be Santa Claus? Perhaps it was. It seemed that anything was possible. His first thought had been that he would have to pay for that himself.

"It just so happens," Will Brady said, "that I'm more or less alone at Christmas."

"I can understand that," Mrs. Beach replied, as her own children were gone and seldom came around, as they all had children of their own. Nor was there any chance of her, plump as she was, of pretending she was Santa Claus. She was simply not the type—whatever that might be.

The retail store of Montgomery Ward & Co., where they were looking for a Santa Claus, was right where the drawbridge crossed the sewage canal. So it was not any trouble for Will Brady to just stop by, as he said. To inquire what it was they had in mind for a Santa Claus. But as he entered the store the main aisle was obstructed by ten or twelve people, gathered in an arc, facing a corner with a well-lighted display. There was a comfortable chair, of the reclining type, several lamps with large aluminum shades, and a young man with taffy-colored hair and a deeply tanned face. He wore a clean white jacket of the type Will Brady had seen on dentists and doctors, and held in his tanned right hand a long wand. With this wand, as he talked, he pointed at the statements on a large poster, which included a detailed, cut-away picture of one of the lamps. The name of the lamp was NU-VITA, which meant new life.

The voice of the young man was pleasant, and he had that healthy outdoor look that city people, like Will Brady himself, liked to gaze upon. It might be that Will Brady was reminded of his son. Not that there was any particular resemblance— this boy was older, larger, and blond—but Will Brady saw the boy whenever he saw the outdoor type. The athlete who still wore his study glasses, so to speak. As the young man talked, in his persuasive voice, Will Brady read the statements on the poster and discovered that the lamp he saw on the platform was a marvelous thing, a lamp that trapped the sun, so to speak. That gave off the same life-giving rays of light. These rays gave plants the color of green, and man the life-giving coat of tan. The city dweller, the young man was saying, lived little better than the life of a mole, but science had now discovered how to bring the sun right into his room. Right into his attic, if that was where he lived. With this wonderful lamp he could sit at home—reading a book, or just resting with his clothes off—and absorb the mysterious life-giving rays of the sun. Without the sun there would be nothing on earth—nothing but cold rocks and fish-less seas. But with the sun there was light, plants, and creatures like themselves. And with this lamp a man could have the sun with him anywhere.

Perhaps it was the sun-tanned face of the young man—the very picture of life, if Will Brady had ever seen it—that led the old man in the aisle to gaze at him in a certain way. Perhaps it was this gaze, somehow, that attracted the young man. Whatever it was, he suddenly stopped talking, turned the wand he was holding from the poster, and pointed it over the heads of those who stood at the front. Pointed it, that is, at Will Brady himself.

"Will the gentleman," the young man said, "be so kind as to please step forward? Will the gentleman allow me, without cost or the slightest obligation, to demonstrate?"

It would be wrong to say that Will Brady followed all of this. He saw the pointer, he heard the young man's voice, he felt the eyes of those assembled upon him, and when those at the front made way, why, he stepped to the front. He took a seat in the reclining chair that was prepared for him. A white bib, like a barber's cloth, was placed upon his front. Then his head was raised—through it all he heard the clear, calm voice of the attendant —and a pair of dark glasses was placed over his eyes, tied at the back. For a moment he saw all before him darkly, as if submerged in muddy water; then he was tipped back, and as his head went down, his feet went up. Over his head appeared the wide shade, he watched the adjustment of the black carbons, heard the hum of the current, then the crackling as the flame leaped the arc. A burning smell, perhaps the breath of life itself, made him wrinkle his nose.

"If the gentleman will kindly lid his eyes," said the voice, and as the crackling spread into a glow, Will Brady felt himself in a warm, colorless bath of light. The odor of the carbon was strong in his nose, and the flavor in his mouth. But he felt no fear; in the words of the voice, now disembodied, that he heard above him, he felt himself "cleansed of pollutions and invigorated from head to toe." The life-giving rays, as the voice went on to say, were mingling with his blood.

He felt suspended—out of this world, as he described it to Bessie Muller—and then, just as he was reborn, the power went off. For a moment he felt that his own worldly system had come to a stop. He made as if to rise, he gasped for air, but the young man's firm hand pressed him back, removed the white cloth, and then slipped the glasses from his head. As he sat up, blinking, the young man said: "You will notice the healthy touch of color that the life-giving rays have given to the gentleman's face."

And so they did, as he saw them nodding, their eyes filled with wonder, as they gazed on what it had done to him. For himself, he could feel the tightness in his cheeks. "That was but a moment," the young man was saying. "If the gentleman could spare me more of his time—just a few moments a day—he would soon be as sun-tanned as myself." So saying, he rolled up his sleeve, showed the brown arm. He smiled, showing in his dark face the firm white teeth. Then he assisted Will Brady to his feet, putting into his right hand, as he did so, a wide selection of charts concerned with what the Nu-Vita would do for him. It could also be purchased, as he pointed out, on the easy-payment plan. His own brown hand on Will Brady's shoulder, he called everyone's attention to his fine, healthy look, and asked him, when he found the time, to drop by again. A few more treatments, as he said, and he wouldn't recognize himself.

In this rejuvenated condition Will Brady found himself in the aisle, and he wandered about, from counter to counter, for some time. He seemed to have forgotten why he had entered the store. He stopped to gaze, wherever it was reflected, at his own new face. It was different. There was no doubt about that. Around the eyes he was whiter, but the warm cheeks were pink. Rosy? Well, there was even a touch of that. His own yellow teeth seemed to look whiter when he smiled. In this condition he sought out the man at the back of the store—a Mr. Nash—and inquired of him what they had in mind for Santa Claus. Mr. Nash, looking at him soberly, begged him to have a seat.

What they had in mind, Mr. Nash said, speaking to him very frankly, was no monkey business. They had to be sure of that. While he was on the job he had to be Santa Claus, nobody else. Having said this, Mr. Nash looked at him, and what he saw in the new pink face before him seemed to be what he wanted, seemed to be a Santa Claus that he could trust. One that he could turn over, as he said, their reputation to. He had on file other applications, but if Will Brady wanted the job he would take him upstairs and show him the setup, give him the suit. All that he would have to dig up himself was a kid to blow the balloons.

"To blow what?" Will Brady said.

He would need a kid to blow the balloons. He would give away balloons, but he would need some kid to blow them up. The kid sat under the throne, under the seat, that is, where Santa Claus would be sitting, and after blowing up the balloon he would pass it between his legs. That was how they did it. He would have to find the kid to do that himself.

In the Wasteland

Will Brady said that he would think it over—if he could find the right boy, he would surely think it over—and on his way through the store he passed a new crowd of people around the sun lamp. The young man with the pointer, seeing him pass, waved the wand at him.

"There goes a satisfied user, right there," he said, "it has made that gentleman look years younger," and everyone in the crowd, half the people in the aisle, turned to look at him. He smiled, he felt the strain of trying to throw his shoulders back. He reached the street, he crossed the bridge, he made his way through the freight yards and into the tower room, before he noticed that he still held the literature in his hand.

"Plug in at home or office," it said, and he read that the small model in question, meant to sit on a table, could be had for just four dollars a month.

On the first Monday in December, following another successful free trial, Will Brady purchased a desk-model sun lamp, carrying it along with him, in its carton, as he left the store. The warm glow of the lamp, in the crisp night air, was still there on his face. Mrs. Plinski had remarked the new look to his face, which she thought was due to the brisk fall weather, and after thinking it over he decided to let it go at that. Woman that she was, she might find it hard to understand something like the Nu-Vita, a marvel that brought the sun, so to speak, right into the house. And along with it the crackling sound, and the crisp frying smell. As he could plug it in either at home or at the office, he decided on the office as he could be alone, day or night, in the tower room. He could give himself a treatment, as it was called, any time that he got around to it, which turned out to be two or three times a night. Once when he arrived, as a rule, and then again when he left. He would clear one corner of the table of waybills, take off his vest, his tie, and his shirt, then open his underwear so that some of the rays fell on his chest. The only problem he faced was in keeping the time, as it passed very fast. Five to seven minutes were supposed to be enough. But seated there in the glow, like a warm bath, it was hard to keep from dozing off, or thinking thoughts that he could time or bring to a stop. With the dark glasses on he found it hard to read his watch. So he may have slipped over now and then, but not that it mattered, as he had only five days to prepare himself as Santa Claus.

As Santa Claus he wore a red cotton flannel suit, loose in the seat and very long in the arms, a pair of black rubber boots, and a soiled, strong-smelling beard. He sat on a throne, which in turn was on a platform, between two large cardboard reindeer, one of them with electric eyes that sparked on and off. At the back of the throne was the room where he dressed, hung up his clothes, and walked out on the fire escape, now and then, for a breath of fresh air. Under the throne was Manny Plinski, seated on a stool. In his lap he held a large bag of Christmas balloons, and at his side, in a glass jar, the baby turtles he had brought along to keep him company.

When Santa Claus wanted a balloon he would tap with his heel on the throne, and Manny Plinski would blow one up and pass it to him. Sometimes, however, he handed Santa Claus a baby turtle instead. As you can't risk passing out live turtles to little city boys who had never seen one, Santa Claus would have to slip these turtles into the pocket of his coat. Toward the end of the day he might have more than his pockets would hold. He would have to get up and take out the sign reading:

MAKING DELIVERY
Santa Claus Back Soon

and go through the side door and speak to Manny Plinski, personally. There were times when Manny Plinski was ashamed and took it all right. There were other times when he giggled, ran his hands like a rake through his yellow hair, and passed up another turtle as soon as he laid his hands on one.

263 '

These times Santa Claus would have to rap his knuckles, or sprinkle him with some water from the empty turtle jug on the floor. That sometimes did it; other times it didn't work out too well. He would blow up balloons and sit there popping them with his teeth.

Another thing that Manny Plinski liked to do was take the brown tweed suit that belonged to Will Brady and fill the pockets with turtles and balloons. He seemed to like the brown suit better than he liked Santa Claus. He liked to take the brown suit and go off alone somewhere and sit with it. Santa Claus would have to stop and hunt him down, as he couldn't blow balloons for himself, but this wasn't too often, and Manny Plinski was never far. He was usually out on the fire escape, just sitting there. He like to watch the trains shifting around in the freight yards, and the boats on the canal. He would blow Christmas balloons, like bubbles, and let them drift away.

Not that it seemed to matter, as there were plenty of balloons, plenty of time to stop and look for him, and the old man in the Santa Claus suit seemed to like his work. He would have paid Montgomery Ward & Co. in order to carry on with it. Out on the street an old man cannot hold hands with children, bounce them on his knee, or tell them lies that he will not be responsible for. Nor can he bend his head and let them whisper into his ear. Very much as if he, this old man, could do something for them. Very much as if he knew, like the children before him, that there was only one man in this world—one man still living—who was prepared to do certain things. To live in this world, so to speak, and yet somehow be out of it. To be himself without children, without friends or relations, without a woman of his own or a past or a future, and yet to be mortal, and immortal, at the same time. Only one man in the world could answer an ad worded like that. Only one man, that is, and get away with it. For in the world it is evil for an old man to act like that. There is a law against it—unless the old man is Santa Claus. But for this old man these things are all right, they are recognized to be the things that count; and the children, as they do in such cases, all believe in him. Some men will put up with a good deal, from certain quarters, for a job like that.

"Oh, how they will love you!" Mrs. Plinski said, and every day his cheeks seemed a little redder, his smile a little brighter, and the face in the mirror no longer his own. It had become, it seemed to him, the face of Santa Claus. Only the eyes, with the white circles around them, were still his own. They were there because of the goggles, and the darker his face seemed to get, the redder his cheeks, the more pale and sallow his eyes. So he began to move

the goggles up and down, first to one side, then to
the other, and one evening he tried it without the
goggles for a little bit. It wouldn't matter, he felt
sure, if he kept his eyes closed. Nothing came of
that, so the next evening he tried it a little longer,
and was pleased to find that the white cricles were
getting pink. They began to blend in, a little more,
with the rest of his face. So he tried it again, this
time a little longer, as it was past the middle of December, and Santa Claus had before him only one
more week.

That was the morning of December 19, but it
was late in the afternoon, the daylight gone, before
his eyes began to smart. They watered a little, and
the lids were red when he looked at them. He had
to buy a handkerchief in the store and keep dabbing
at his eyes when he stopped for supper, and he
noticed that the boy, Manny Plinski, kept staring
at him. Sometimes he would whimper as if he
wasn't feeling good. In the evening the lights
seemed to make it worse, and he had to stop, every
half hour or so, to step back behind the curtain
where it was dark and press the lids shut. When
he did that, he found it hard to open them. The
salty liquid that kept running seemed to make them
stick. Something in the lids seemed to draw them
closed, so that he had to stare to hold them open,
but all the time, without letup, the tears ran down

his face. Around his red, peeling nose the skin was very tender, smarting when he wiped his cheeks, and he thought he detected in the handkerchief the burned-carbon smell. As if the rays that had soaked into him were now sweating out.

Later he put up the sign; he found it hard to recognize the little boys from the girls, and to open his eyes he had to use his fingers, separate the lids. The inside of the lids was bright red, like the gills of a fish. When he removed his fingers, the lower lids would roll up, as a curtain rolls. Nothing he could do, even with his fingers, would put a stop to this. For air, for fresh cool air, as that in the room seemed to blow hot on his eyeballs, he walked to the back and opened the door to the fire escape. It was snowing a little, and the sharp, cold pricks felt good on his face. He opened the door and stepped out on the landing, facing the freight yards, the sluggish canal, and the blinking traffic that passed on Halsted Street. The water in the canal looked like pig iron poured out to cool. Rising from the water, like a dark-red planet, was the lantern on the drawbridge, and beyond the arc of the bridge he could see the tower room. The light was on. He had probably forgotten it. Beyond the bridge, and the sluggish water, were the smoke and steel of the freight yards, where a brakeman, waving his lantern, walked along the cars. Beyond this, as if a fire was raging, there was a bright glow over the street, and from these flames there arose, along with the din, a penetrating smell. The old man let his eyes close, as this was not something he needed to see. He could breathe it, like the carbon, he could taste it on his lips. It was like the grating sound of steel, a blend of the sour air and the track sound, of the gas from the traffic, and the sweetish smell of powdered Christmas balloons. All of the juices of the city were there on the fire, and brought to a boil. All the damp air of the chill rooms that were empty, the warm soiled air of the rooms that were lived in, blown to him, so it seemed, by the bellows of hell. An acrid stench, an odor so bad that it discolored paint, corroded metal, and shortened the life of every living thing that breathed it in. But the old man on the landing inhaled it deeply, like the breath of life. He leaned there on the railing, his eys closed, but on his face the look of a man with a vision—a holy man, one might even say, as he was feeding the birds. But when the lantern dropped down, and the traffic flowed again, he did a strange thing. He went down the turning stairs toward the water, toward the great stench as if he would grasp it, make it his own, before it could blow away from him. Or as if he heard above the sound of the traffic, the trains in the yard, and the din of the city, the tune of that Piper—the same old Pied Piper—over the canal.

In the Wasteland

The one that had drawn him, time and again, into the streets. So he went on down, groping a little, as he had no proper eyes for seeing, or for knowing that there was no landing over the canal. A rope swung there, the knotted end sweeping the water, heavy with ice.

There was no one on the stairs, nor any boat on the water, and only Manny Plinski, with a brown tweed coat, was there on the landing when they came to look for Santa Claus. In the pockets there were turtles and a postcard to his son that had not been mailed.